ynn, who would become Robin Hood, looked about and then motioned them to come closer. He dropped his voice to a whisper. "These rubies cannot fall into John's hands. They will help put a villain on the throne of England. He will use them to buy an army to achieve his goal. Anything we can do to stop that is good."

"Maybe the rubies could help more people," Hubie said.

Listening to both Fynn and Hubie, an idea began to form in Matty's mind.

HAWKSMAID

THE UNTOLD STORY OF
ROBIN HOOD AND MAID MARIAN

KATHRYN LASKY

HARPER

An Imprint of HarperCollins*Publishers*

Library of Congress Cataloging-in-Publication Data

Lasky, Kathryn.

Hawksmaid : the untold story of Robin Hood and Maid Marian / Kathryn Lasky. — 1st ed.

p.   cm.

Summary: In twelfth-century England, Matty grows up to be a master falconer, able to communicate with the devoted birds who later help her and Fynn, also known as Robin Hood, to foil Prince John's plot to steal the crown.

ISBN 978-0-06-000072-1

1. Maid Marian (Legendary character)—Juvenile fiction. 2. Robin Hood (Legendary character)—Juvenile fiction. 3. Great Britain—History—John, 1199–1216—Juvenile fiction. [1. Maid Marian (Legendary character)—Fiction. 2. Falconry—Fiction. 3. Birds of prey—Fiction. 4. Human-animal relationships—Fiction. 5. Robin Hood (Legendary character)—Fiction. 6. Middle Ages—Fiction. 7. Great Britain—History—John, 1199–1216—Fiction.]   I. Title.

PZ7.L3274Haw   2010   2009024097

[Fic]—dc22   CIP

                                                                 AC

Typography by Hilary Zarycky

11   12   13   14   15   CG/CW   10 9 8 7 6 5 4 3 2 1

❖

First paperback edition, 2011

CONTENTS

HAWKSMAID

BOOK ONE

WHEN ROBIN HOOD WAS FYNN

and

WHEN MAID MARIAN WAS MATTY

PROLOGUE

A hawk will never serve a tyrant.

"TRAITORS!" THE ANGUISH IN her father's voice tore into Matty as sharply as any dagger. "They've cut the hoistings. We can't raise the drawbridge! It's sabotage!"

Lord William Fitzwalter had just run from the drawbridge through the bailey into the castle's great hall and up two flights of stairs to his private chamber. His face was drawn into a pale mask of shock. Moments before, he had witnessed the last of his peasants frantically driving their sheep and pigs before them across the drawbridge to seek refuge, only to be denied safety.

Matty shuddered as her father looked at her mother,

his eyes misted. "I can't believe it, Suzanne."

"Neither can I, William, you—Richard's staunchest supporter."

"That's just the problem," her father cried. "I sided with Richard the Lionhearted and not with his brother. Prince John is behind this, and John's lackey the—"

"The sheriff!" Hodge, her father's oldest and most faithful servant, exclaimed. "It's the sheriff all right, and Sir Guy of Gisborne with him."

"No! Guy of Gisborne!" Lady Suzanne gasped, her shudder running through Matty.

"Hide, Suzanne! Hide, Matty!" her father shouted. "Have they struck at any other castles?"

"I daresay we're the first to be hit," Hodge said.

"First, second, matters not—there will be more," Lord William shouted, his voice hoarse with desperation. "Suzanne, don't dally. Hide!"

Matty's mother pressed her so close that her bodice lacings dug into Matty's cheeks. Matty was eye-to-eye with the pendant that her mother always wore. The jewel, set in a filigree of finely wrought gold, was a midnight-blue star sapphire. *If I just keep looking into this deep-blue stone, we shall be safe*, Matty thought. *It will be the sky, and we will be little stars and float away.*

Dear God, save us. She told herself, *Keep looking at the star . . . the Star of Jerusalem.*

Was she praying or bargaining with God? Perhaps she herself wasn't even sure. She knew only that she wanted to live, for no one to be hurt. But already she could hear the distant thunder of hooves of big horses, coursers and warhorses—horses trained to charge through hordes of defenseless people. They rarely flinched, never shied. They destroyed.

The horses, ever closer, were pounding on the hard ground on the far side of the moat. Matty tried to blot out the fear.

She kept her eyes fixed on the jewel. The milky streaks of light in most sapphires' blue domes formed a star, but in this one the vertical rays had elongated to suggest a cross. Matty's father had given the Star of Jerusalem to his wife in celebration of Matty's birth. In another week, on September 23, she would turn ten. "Please, dear Lord, let me live to ten," she whispered into her mother's breast.

"William," she heard her mother say, "my jewel casket."

"Forget the jewels. Matty is our only jewel. Hide her!"

"Where?"

"The kitchen! The potato hole! I don't know where. Just hide."

He was out the door and calling for his men. Matty could hear shouts; then the hoofbeats became deafening. As the horses crossed the drawbridge, even the floor on which she stood began to shake. The sheriff's men had arrived!

"Quick, Matty, to the kitchens!" Lady Suzanne pulled Matty with one hand and with the other began to fumble with a bracelet. They ran down the twisting steps and across a small service yard to the kitchen house.

Crouching on the earthen floor near the huge oven where a pig was still turning on a spit, they dragged the cover off the potato hole. Her mother reached in and began hauling out potatoes and other root vegetables.

"I'll never fit, Mother. Never. I'm bigger than a potato. Bigger than a sack of potatoes." There was a clatter just outside and then the glint of chain mail flashed in the sunlight. Matty and her mother exchanged horrified glances. Her mother's fingers locked on the necklace. "Mother, the necklace might fit but not me!"

Lady Suzanne blinked. "You're right." She began tearing off her rings. "Run, Matty! Run!"

Matty streaked out the kitchen's back door. She was running toward a small tower between the dog kennels and the stables in the bailey. Around her in the enclosed courtyard men on horseback were clashing with the remaining servants and few loyal vassals, the villeins, or tenant landholders, of Lord William. Squealing pigs and goats were dashing everywhere. The smoke from the burning wattle-and-daub huts surrounding the castle thickened as gusting winds drove it across the drawbridge and into the courtyard. Dogs were barking, hens were clucking, and the courtyard was swirling with frightened animals.

Matty had but one thought: she must get to the tower mews where the hawks were kept. If she could get to them, the birds would keep her safe. She felt this in the deepest part of her being. Her father was a master·falconer, the best in the shire—some said the best in all England. These thoughts streamed through her head and then everything stopped.

The most immense horse she had ever seen was bearing down on her. Its ears were laid back, nostrils flared. She was frozen to the ground. The rider was not reining him in! The words came to her almost idly. *He is not going to stop. I am going to die.*

Then suddenly there was a terrible squeal as the horse swerved to avoid hitting a pig. Matty broke from her daze and ran into the mews tower.

The mews with its few narrow windows was a dim, shadowy place, but the shadows never seemed really dark. The moment she entered she felt wrapped in a fragile golden light like a radiant mist that seemed to settle around her. What was it about the mews? she often wondered. It seemed to transform the simplest things, like stone and wood and the very air one breathed, into something different. When she crossed the threshold, she felt as if she had entered another world.

There were three levels. The six hawks were kept on the first because it afforded the most room for their perches and the other necessities for tending their needs. As soon as she ran in Matty could tell the birds, some hooded, were agitated. Tethered to their perches by supple leather strips called jesses, they roused their wings futilely, making screeching cries of alarm.

Matty's heart was pounding as loudly as the horse hooves outside, but she could hear Moss, the peregrine, making low, guttural noises deep in her throat. The sounds soothed Matty. She felt her own heart quiet, and she could tell that the other birds were beginning to listen to Moss as well.

Matty swallowed and tried to imitate these sounds. They reminded her of small pebbles rubbing together. Her first attempts were not successful. But gradually she felt the sounds forming. Soon she heard them coming from her own throat. Moss's dark eyes were like two polished black stones ringed in yellow. The peregrine nodded as if to say *continue*. Matty did and soon heard Moss's soothing sounds blending with her own. A calm seeped into the mews.

Still making the gurgling sounds, Matty crept toward one of the small windows and peered out. She caught her breath. "No!" she whispered. A catapult had been wheeled to the center of the bailey. She saw her father being led forward. In the short space of time, he had become an old man. His mouth hung slack; his eyes were unseeing. Next to him was a man whose rich clothes proclaimed him to be Sir Guy of Gisborne. A thin strand dangled from his fingers. It seemed to be dripping and red. Something sparkled, a glint of gold in the last flare of the day's sun. A disorganized jumble of images jostled in Matty's mind. *A ruby necklace? No, Mother doesn't have rubies.*

Then the sun in its last spasm delivered a dagger of light, and Matty saw what Gisborne held. Her mother's necklace! The Star of Jerusalem's blue blazed. The gold chain dripped with the blood from her mother's throat.

As Matty retched and moaned, Moss's wing brushed softly over her shoulder. The peregrine had flown down from her perch as far as her jesses would permit. There was a deathly quiet in the bailey. Then a creaking sound—the catapult—and a tortured sob. "My wife murdered. What next? My king? Where is my king?"

But beneath her father's anguished cry there was another voice, an elusive whispering deep in her mind. She turned and looked at Moss. It was as if the peregrine were trying to actually say something to her. It was one thing to imitate the birds, but could Matty ever understand their meaning?

She turned back to the scene in the courtyard in time to see Sir Guy's face redden with anger. "Richard is not king yet. Nor will he be."

"His eldest brother has died. He is the next in line after the old king dies," Lord William said defiantly.

"Swear allegiance now to Prince John."

"Never!" Lord William spat out the single word.

Gisborne's eyes glittered, then a sly smile like a knife blade split his face. He gave a signal to the sheriff. Matty inhaled sharply as she saw the sheriff's men turn the catapult on the mews tower.

"Prince John," bellowed the sheriff, "has heard of your hawks. If you will not give him the peregrine and swear fealty to the prince, we have orders to destroy the mews."

"I could deliver my hawk, but Prince John will never master her. A hawk will never serve a tyrant! Moss is faithful to me. I am the one who raised her. A hawk is faithful to the one who has reared it with love and temperance!"

"That remains to be seen," the sheriff replied. His men drew back the arm of the catapult.

Matty's heart raced. *What would Fynn do? Something clever, no doubt.* It might have proven more dangerous than clever when Fynn, the month before, had stolen the eggs and also a royal forester's wife's prize hen. Fynn hadn't kept the eggs for himself but given them to poor Nanny Wodehouse. The hen . . . well, no one knew exactly what had happened to the hen, but somewhere she was still laying, and every now and then her eggs appeared in the wattle huts of the poorest people in the village. Only Matty knew that Fynn was responsible for this bit of mischief, or at least she hoped she was the only one. *So what would Fynn do in the face of a catapult trained squarely on the mews?*

Then once more she heard a whispering deep in the back of her mind. She tipped her head to one side and looked at Moss. The peregrine cocked her own head and looked back at her, murmuring—no, not at her but into her. The bird's sound and vision seemed to go beyond her skin, beyond the human form and body that was recognized as Matilda Fitzwalter. She felt the shadow of another being stir inside her. *Something is happening,* Matty thought, *something very odd.*

Then she rose as if in a trance.

"I am to set you all free. That is the message!" Matty felt a wild joy at this sudden insight. It was as if the barriers between human and bird had suddenly dissolved.

She rushed toward the snug corner where the hawking tools were kept. Among the various instruments were several small knives. She seized one and, just as the first large stone hit the tower, she cut the jesses off Moss. She worked quickly, cutting jesses and unhooding those birds who wore them. Then she ran about, flailing her arms, shooing them toward the upper windows. "Go! Go!"

Stones pounded against the tower walls. The sound was deafening. The air seemed to convulse. She pressed her hands to her ears and screamed, "Go! Go! Fly away!"

She watched as they spread their wings. She felt windy drafts as they roused in preparation for lifting off. If she could only fly! Fly away from this castle where her mother had just been murdered, away from this shire with its monstrous sheriff, away from this island realm called England. "Why did you leave us, Richard? Why? Why?" She screamed the question that ricocheted in her brain as the stones pounded the tower. Why had this knightly prince left them all to his monstrous brother and the fiendish sheriff? *Fiends! Fiends!* Fiends sent in to destroy her home, her family's castle! Matilda Fitzwalter looked up as the walls of the tower began to crumble around her and she saw the last of the birds fly out. *They're free!*

Chapter 1

FIRST LESSONS

*Hawking is not about the flight or the kill but about the
bond between the falconer and the bird.*

THE HAWKS HAD COME back as Lord William had
predicted—not all of them, but four returned.
"The stalwarts," he called them. Moss had been
the first, flying into the chapel during Lady Suzanne's
funeral. Matty had not attended; she was unconscious
from being knocked on the head by fragments of the
mews walls. Hodge's wife, old Meg, hovered around
her bed for endless hours. Nelly Woodfynn, mother of
Fynn, was there as well. She had come to help nurse,
and Fynn paced anxiously nearby.

Matty had been lying motionless for nearly two
days, her lips drained of color, her eyelids so swollen

that barely a quiver could be detected. But after his wife's burial, Lord William had taken the peregrine into the chamber, and Matty began to rouse.

"Look, my lord!" Fynn cried as Moss flew to perch on Matty's bed. "Her eyelids are fluttering!"

"Robert, I believe you're right." Lord William never called Matty's friend Fynn but by his proper Christian name. His father was the warden of the woods of Barnsdale. Fynn, who was a year and a half older than Matty, had played with her at the castle when his parents had come there on business. Lord William often gave them food from the larder in exchange for Nelly's nursing his family and servants. She was known to be the best midwife in the shire and one of the few who would treat lepers.

Fynn stepped closer to the bed. "She's coming around, my lord, I tell you. She's trying to say something."

"Free . . . free," Matty kept muttering. Her face was bruised more colors of purple than Fynn had ever seen. One eye was swollen completely shut. Above the other was a yellowish bump the size of a hen's egg. But by some miracle Matty had survived with no broken bones.

Perched on the bedstead, Moss began making

strange guttural sounds. A hush fell across the room. Everyone sensed a further quickening of Matty's slumbering spirit beneath the lumps and bumps and bruises. "Free . . . free," Matty said more clearly. And then the words stopped, replaced by a slow gurgling sound from back of her throat.

"She can't breathe!" Fynn lurched toward the slight form in the bed. Lord William shot out his arm and stayed him as Moss raised her feathers threateningly and then in one quick hop landed on Matty's pillow. It was an odd picture, the long deadly talons digging into the soft goose down. But Matty's eyes suddenly opened.

"You came back!" she whispered to the peregrine. "You came back!"

Within hours, one by one, the other birds arrived: Morgana the kestrel, Ulysses the goshawk, and Lyra the short-winged hawk. They came back to their master, Lord William Fitzwalter, whose wife had been murdered; whose silver and gold and jewels had been stolen; whose larder had been emptied; whose fields had been burned; and whose servants, peasants, and vassals had gone. But most of his hawks had come back.

* * *

Fynn started to bring some of his friends to visit while Matty recovered.

She liked Fynn's friends and found their company lively. There was Rich Much, the miller's son; Hubert Bigge, whose father was dead but whose mother was a brewer; and a handsome boy called Will Scarloke, son of the blacksmith. A few days later, Matty was even able to laugh when Fynn said, "Your face looks like a few squashed plums, and that egg over your eye—well, it's gone down, more like a fried egg now." The boys talked about roaming the forest of Barnsdale, hunting, fishing, and "adventuring," as they called it. Matty longed to get well enough to join them.

It was while she was still propped up in her bed that Matty had her first falconry lesson. What was remarkable about this lesson was the way in which her father spoke to her.

"Matilda," he began gravely, "we have lost so much. But we will live through these terrible times. A tyrant will not vanquish us. The rightful heir will return; and when Richard does, we will be prepared to serve him. But we must *live* to do that. The hawks will help us survive. I am going to teach you how to take care of them and how to gain their trust and become a master falconer. I am getting older. I can't run with the hawks the way I once did. You are young, strong, and smart."

Matty was astonished. She had never heard anyone speak of a girl in quite this way. He looked at her seriously and said, "I am counting on you."

"How do you take care of them, Father?" she asked.

"You must learn, first of all, to see to their health in general and to the health of their feathers especially. Let's start with imping."

"Imping?"

"Imping—mending the broken feathers of injured hawks."

It was a good first lesson. Hawks often damaged their feathers when hunting, and three of the returning hawks had suffered feather injuries. Every falconer kept a supply of molted feathers for the sole purpose of repairing broken ones. Luckily, Lord William's box of feathers in the mews had not been destroyed when the upper part of the tower collapsed.

So Matty learned how to whittle a molted feather's shaft so it could be grafted to the remains of the damaged one that still grew from the injured bird. She learned to use an imping needle to insert the new feather into the quill of the damaged one, and to fix it in place with a special paste. It was delicate work, and as she learned she felt herself begin to mend.

The first feather she imped was for Ulysses, a fierce and fearless bird. He had broken a tail covert.

"He'll need that one done well. You'll see, Matty. Ulysses is an expert in flying in tight spaces. A goshawk can follow prey through a maze of shrubs and thick brush, but he must have his tail for steering." The immense bird nearly covered half her bed but was quite patient as Matty carefully worked. "You'll begin to understand all this, Matty. You'll see that to really know how a hawk flies you have to learn to think like a hawk."

Think like a hawk! When her father had said those words six months ago, she had blinked in confusion. The words hinted at some kind of magical transformation. And, indeed, it did seem as though there was an end to the tedious life of being a girl who could prepare only for marriage. It would not matter if she could embroider a lovely altar cloth for the castle chapel or learn to dance the saltarello, which her mother claimed to have danced so superbly that she had captivated half a dozen noblemen, including Lord William. Within the space of a very short time, a time of deprivation that most considered terrible, Matilda Fitzwalter's life changed completely . . . and she loved it.

During the long winter nights her father taught her how to play chess. She began to learn how to read, a skill considered most unfeminine. What man would ever want anything to do with a girl so clever she could read? Maidens were supposed to read—if at all—the Bible. But Lord William had a book on falconry and it was no time before Matty needed not only to read that book but also to write. Lately, she'd begun to learn how to hunt with her father and to keep meticulous records. She made observations of how the hawks flew, how they plunged, or stooped, in for a kill. Did they favor the left wing or the right? It was important to know their habits, their preferences. Matty wrote it all down.

Matty and her father, each with a hawk on the shoulder, walked the fields beyond the castle walls on this chill March day. Her eyes surveyed the muddy ground for any signs of game. As her father had predicted, falconry was no longer simply a sport for them. They were dependent on the hawks for food. The raids ordered by Prince John and carried out by the sheriff of Nottingham and Sir Guy of Gisborne had depleted Lord William's coffers. The other nobles throughout the shire who were not in league with the prince could not help. They were also under attack. Lord William began selling the few castle treasures he had left—tapestries, jewels, art. His small herd of cows had stopped giving milk because they were starving. Then the flocks of chickens began to thin out. Now all the animals were gone except the hawks.

Game was scarce where Matty and her father were walking and she wished they could go farther, but her father could not manage great distances since the raid. And he was not about to let Matty go abroad alone. This morning she wore a falconer's gauntlet on her left arm, and Moss the peregrine's talons encircled the glove almost completely. Lord William looked at his daughter proudly. She was learning so quickly. This was only her third or fourth time out flying a hawk since she had regained her strength after that horrendous day.

As they crossed the field, Matty sensed a new

alertness in Moss. The peregrine shifted her weight on the glove. A riffle ran through the sleek black cap of feathers on her head, and her shoulder coverts stirred. Matty's father never spoke as she prepared to launch a hawk in flight. That had been part of the first lessons.

"I shall remain quiet, Matilda, when you are practicing launching. No man can tell another when a bird is fit to take flight."

"I'm not a man, Father! I'm a girl."

"Sorry, sorry. You will be the finest *falconress* in England."

"No, just call me a falconer. No special word." She paused and gave him a mischievous look. "But do remember I'm a girl."

"How could I ever forget?" There was a sudden light in Lord William's rheumy eyes. She knew that she was the cause, the jewel that was the source of this sparkle. She didn't much like being thought of as a jewel any more than she enjoyed being called a falconress. But she was happy that her father seemed to have regained some of his former spirit.

Moss stirred again on her arm. With her right hand Matty started undoing the jesses. The peregrine began to make subtle movements signaling that she was in hunting order. Matty opened her mouth slightly and made a rough sawlike sound. This was the first thing that had astounded Lord William. He himself had hawked for nearly a half century but had never been able to master that back-of-the-throat language in which hawks often communicated. She was now readying Moss for the loft, not simply through her body's motions but through language—a language Lord William had once believed was inaccessible to humans. And he knew that Matty was becoming more fluent each day. He often caught her speaking to herself as if practicing. Sometimes he almost felt that she was not merely thinking like a hawk but was herself part hawk.

Matty threw her left arm up. A high, shrill noise pealed from Moss's throat as she spotted a duck rising from a grassy hummock. The hawk was in the air, her great wings spread against the flawless blue sky. Matty and her father squinted as they followed the course of the bold assassin. Their hearts raced as they saw Moss begin to fold her wings. This was the moment of truth, the dive of a peregrine, a moment unmatched by anything else in hunting. Moss took her prey in a steep vertical stoop, putting on a cunning burst of speed. The dagger points of her talons struck, blood splattered the sky. The duck died instantly.

"She's binding to it!" her father whispered excitedly.

Moss gripped the duck as they tumbled to the ground together—rather gently considering the ferocity of the attack. A trail of duck feathers streamed in their wake. Matty felt a sudden dizziness. Just for a second or two, it was almost as if she *herself* were tumbling through the air. And once again the boundaries that separated human beings from birds seemed to dissolve. *If I can feel this, couldn't I . . . ?* But she dared not wonder. The very thought seemed too bold to consider.

Moss was not Matty's only avian teacher. Each hawk—be it a short-winged hawk like Lyra, a kestrel like Morgana, or a goshawk like Ulysses—had his or her own style of flying and hunting. Matty needed to learn them all. While Moss brought down the duck, Ulysses perched on Lord William's shoulder. With his pale gray plumage the immense goshawk seemed to hover like a ghost. He was the largest of all the hawks and a commanding presence even when hooded. Ulysses had not been flown since Matty had imped his tail feathers when she was still recovering. But her father had brought him today.

Matty was nervous. This would be the true test of her skills. Would the imped feather hold? Her father had said that she had done a good job, but it wasn't just the feather that made her worry. She had not yet worked with a goshawk but knew Ulysses's style was to search for prey in confined spaces, and she had to be patient. One did not launch a goshawk from the glove like a peregrine. Instead, the bird perched above the falconer in a tree, keeping a lookout for prey from a higher vantage point. A goshawk went when he decided the time was right, and in this sense she and Ulysses were not partners. Any distracting motions from the falconer and a goshawk would stubbornly refuse to hunt.

"Now remember what I told you," her father said as he transferred Ulysses to her shoulder. "You can take off his jesses long before you spot anything that might be prey, as long as you remain absolutely still. Ulysses is a bird of uncommon self-discipline—almost what I would call military. It was probably entirely unnecessary for me to have hooded him while you flew Moss."

Matty and her father now followed a hedgerow

that dipped into a meadow. With its thickets and occasional saplings it was an ideal territory for grouse and rabbits.

After she and her father settled under a dense overhang of brush, Matty began to unhood Ulysses. Catching her breath, she felt his piercing red eyes fix her with a commanding gaze. A dark patch of feathers that streamed like a black flame above his eyes made him appear even fiercer as he seemed to say, *Are you prepared, my lady? I am.* Matty prayed that the imped tail feather would not break.

She found that remaining still was the hard part: crouching in dense, prickly brush that poked at her and she could not move to scratch. It was a kind of torture. She hoped the prey wouldn't be a fox. Matty supposed one could eat fox, but she never had and hoped she never would. A plump rabbit would be fine or, better yet, a hare, whose flesh was much richer . She had barely completed the thought when without any warning she felt a great gust.

Ulysses unfolded his enormous wings and flew straight up. Then, like a stone crashing down, he was on track of his prey. Matty's eyes locked on the gray-brown tail of a hare. She watched in awe as Ulysses careened through the dense thickets, swerving and dodging in chase. *The mended feather is working!* Matty followed the swift motions of Ulysses's long tail as he ruddered through the narrow spaces. Although the distance between Matty and the goshawk was increasing, she felt as if something within her was reaching out to him. She sensed every wingbeat as if it were a heartbeat inside her own chest.

"*Ki . . . ki . . . kuh . . . kuh.*" She was urging Ulysses on in the very distinct voice of a goshawk—low, subtle tones that seemed to say *You can do it! Onward!*

Quickly, Ulysses sank his talons into the hare, snapping its neck.

Chapter 2

THE NOTION OF A MERLIN

Learning to fly a hawk for hunting is a continuous process. To really understand how a hawk hunts, one must try to think not only like a hawk but as its quarry.

ULYSSES DROPPED THE HARE at Matty's feet and stepped back, squaring his shoulders. He uttered a brief husky noise, then gave a short nod as if saluting his mistress. Matty nodded back and replied with a similar gravelly utterance.

"Well, Matty!" Lord William exclaimed. "I would say you did right by Ulysses with that imped feather and he's done right by us with this hare."

"Yes, I was glad that the imp didn't break, but the rest of it—his flying—was amazing," Matty replied.

Lord William shook his head in wonder as they headed back to the castle. "Before we lost everything, I had thought of getting a merlin. Too bad we don't have a merlin."

"Why is that, Father?" Matty asked.

"Well, it is said that learning to fly a merlin is what makes the consummate falconer."

"But aren't merlins called pigeon hawks?"

"Yes. It's strange. They are said to be in the same family, but merlins are as unlike pigeons as birds could be. Clever, ambitious, able to feign slowness in flight to fool their prey . . . but they're very difficult to raise. Many people try and then give up and let them loose, but by that time they are ruined. They don't survive very long in the wild when that happens."

"Did you ever have one, Father?"

"Yes, long ago. A bright little fellow. My pride and joy."

"What happened?" Matty asked hesitantly.

Lord William stopped walking. He turned and looked at Matty, his face suddenly grim.

"He was killed?" Matty grew pale. She somehow knew that the bird had not been killed by another animal—had not been taken down in flight by a raptor or sprung upon by a hunting dog—but killed by a human.

"Who?" she whispered.

"Sir Guy of Gisborne." Her father paused. "He seems to kill what he cannot have."

"Kills what he cannot have? What else couldn't he have?"

Lord William stopped, pressed his lips together, and looked at Matty.

"Father, tell me, what else did Sir Guy want and could not have?"

"Your mother, years ago." Lord William bent his head and began to speak rapidly. "He claims that she had been betrothed to him. She wasn't. She hated him and she loved me. In revenge he sent one of his servants to my mews to slay the merlin. Then he had it delivered to us on our wedding day."

Matty gasped. "Fiends, Father. They are all fiends!"

"Yes, and he is Prince John's right-hand man, while the sheriff, I guess one would say, is the left." Lord William resumed walking.

"Father, when will Richard come back? He means to be a good king, doesn't he?"

"Oh, yes, but he is occupied in France, fighting for the lands that belong to him. I have heard that in the past fortnight Prince John has plundered two castles to the north. Some say he even has the *church* in his pocket. You see, Matty, King Henry has grown old and feeble. When he dies, as the youngest son, Prince John has no inheritance while his older brother, Richard, inherits all his father's lands. And John is a very greedy man. As the saying goes, when the cat's away the mice will play."

"But he's a rat!" Matty said. "If you had a son, it would be the same, wouldn't it, and I wouldn't have anything? I mean, that is the custom, isn't it? The oldest son gets everything."

"Well, yes, but you're no rat." Lord William paused. "However, I think I would have to give you my hawks—son or no son."

"You really mean that?" Matty asked.

"I certainly do."

Matty dipped her head and smiled. She felt a surge of deep joy rise within her. "You went to France to fight for Richard and his lands, didn't you—when I was a baby?"

"Yes, twice, once before you were born and once

when you were an infant. I was not the only English-
man who could not tolerate the notion of Prince John
ruling both here and in France. Richard is the better
man. The whole world loves Richard. So what started as
a family squabble became a war—one that we still seem
to be fighting."

That evening when Matty knelt, she prayed for her
mother's soul as she always did. But then she prayed for
more.

"Dear Lord, may good Richard the Lionhearted
come home and make everything right and just and
prosperous again." Then she paused, opened her eyes,
and looked up. She was not sure if it was right to ask
God for the next thing. But the words simply bubbled
up in her like a spring unlocked from winter's ice.
"Dear God, my mother cannot come back and make
me a fine lady, a lady suitable for love and marriage. I
have no dowry for a wedding, but would that I had a
merlin, I could become the finest falconer. Amen."

Chapter 3

THE GREENWOOD

*Falconry is an art and not merely a discipline. If a hawk
has been properly taught, a bond will form between the
teacher and the bird—and then and only then will the
hawk do your bidding and more.*

ATTY CAME OVER THE crest of the hill, knee-
deep in the dry, brown winter grass, the
peregrine on her shoulder. She stopped to
look around and the falcon spread her wings. "*Kush,
Moss! kush nyeep.* . . . Easy, Moss! I'm looking for the
snare."

For the past year, she had learned to hunt with all
the hawks. Her father allowed her finally to go out
alone whenever she liked. The hawks were still their
main means of getting food, but she also got small .

game by setting snares.

The fields, divided by thick hedgerows into squares, spread before her like waves in a patchwork sea. She looked out to where the fields met a dark band on the horizon. The band, which grew thicker and darker, marked the edge of the woods of Barnsdale. This was where Matty longed to be. But first she must check the snare. And then on to the forest, or the greenwood, as it was called when winter finished and the trees leafed.

Matty knew she had set the snare nearby. *It must be here somewhere,* she thought. So foolish of her not to have checked it yesterday. But yesterday she could not leave the castle until well after noon, and then she had been in such a rush to join Fynn and the boys because the weather was finally turning good. The snow, which had lain in frozen thick sheets like a knight's armor, had melted, unlocking the earth from winter's grip. You could *smell* the green. So at last they could all play again. She was anxious to play after such a long, hard, and horrible winter.

It had been one that sucked the life out of people, and if the bitter cold hadn't finished the job, Prince John had. For Matty, who was now eleven, it seemed that her life had been neatly divided into two parts:

before the raid and after the raid. Nothing could have been as awful as that day nearly two years ago when the sheriff and Sir Guy of Gisborne had ridden into their courtyard. But now not only had her father and every village in the shire of Nottingham grown poorer but also Prince John was determined to drain the life blood from this land for his own enrichment. If a lord resisted, his fields were burned and his loyal servants were slain. Peasants were left to starve.

Prince John had an ample supply of henchmen to help him plunder. The sheriff and lords like Sir Guy and others had not only managed to save their own skins by carrying out the prince's orders; they also enriched themselves.

This past month had been particularly harsh. There was not even a single hare to make a hearty stew. Lord William had long ago sold the last of their silver plates, and they now ate like peasants from trenchers, bowls made of hollowed-out stale bread. Matty watched as her father grew thinner and older before her eyes. She, too, had grown thin. That was why it had been careless and selfish of her not to check the snares she had set. But Matty Fitzwalter needed play as much as food. She needed adventure as much as a good, warm cloak.

But most of all she needed her friends on this fine early spring morning She longed to be heading to join the boys deep in the greenwood.

"Where is that snare?" Matty muttered as she searched on the other side of the crest. Moss lighted from her shoulder to the ground. "Where is it?"

Just at that moment she heard a thrashing, followed by a moan. "Right here," a small rabbity voice creaked. "What a snare! You got me!" There was an eruption of snorts and giggles.

"Fynn!"

Fynn popped up from behind the bush. He had shot up several inches and become a gangly lad with wild dark-blond hair that set off the sharp blueness of his eyes. Dry grass stuck out from under his cap. His clothes were splattered with mud, and some winter-burned ferns were tucked here and there. He blended in perfectly with the land. In his hand he held the snare.

"Very funny," Matty said sarcastically. "Was there anything in it besides you?"

"No, sorry. But Rich says there are some grouse flying at the edge of the greenwood. Come on, Matty.

The boys are waiting. The creek is really up. Did you bring your line and hook?"

"Of course." She plunged her hand into a cloth bag that hung from her waist and drew out a neatly coiled line with a hook stabbed into a cork.

"So we can get some fish! And my mum, she sent along some honey."

Well, honey would be nice, Matty thought. What Matty and her father and the two old servants, Hodge and Meg, needed more was some meat.

"And, oh, I nearly forgot. I brought you some pickled pigs' feet." He held up a pouch.

"No! Fynn, you didn't!" Matty's eyes darkened. Pigs were scarce these days. The only pigs that had been slaughtered recently had belonged to the cousin of the sheriff, who raised them for the priory in Barnsdale.

"It's just the feet!"

"You must be off your game if you didn't get the bacon as well. Did you steal it from the sheriff's cousin, or did you march right into the priory?"

"None of your business, Matty. I got it. Now do you want it or not?"

She thought of her father and Meg and Hodge and reached for the pouch. "You know you're going to get caught one of these days, Fynn. Your luck will run out."

"They're not going to discover their loss for a while. I left a nearly identical pouch in its place."

"But an empty one."

"No. I'm too clever for that. Filled it with deer guts. Who's to say it won't be delicious? I might have invented a new dish. Pickled deer guts."

"From a deer you brought down illegally in the royal forest, I suppose." Matty had worried about Fynn's thievery ever since he'd stolen that prize hen and her eggs two years ago. And even though he took only from the well-off to give to most needy, it seemed that his boldness had increased with the value of the goods he plundered. First eggs, now pigs' feet, and before that deer from the royal forest. He was no longer satisfied with a small prize. He left that for the boys. Rich was fairly good with a slingshot, and Will Scarloke could sneak up on a sheriff's man in a crowd on market day and relieve him of a pouch of gold coins without disturbing as much as a thread on the fellow's cuff. What they stole by and large was small, but they were as cunning as any London street cutpurse.

Matty knew that the recent deer was not the first

Fynn had taken, even though his father was a forest
warden. Her family as well as others had been the
recipient of prime cuts of venison that mysteriously
appeared in their larders. She laughed at the memory
of Fynn's face when she had caught him in her larder
during a downpour when no one in their right mind
would have been abroad.

Hunting in the royal forest was punishable by
imprisonment or worse. Often the culprit was tortured
and the torture might include the chopping off of a
finger or two. The sheriff's men and the royal foresters
particularly delighted in separating a hunter from his
bowstring finger. Still, she knew that nothing she could
say would discourage him.

He looked enormously pleased with himself as
he flashed her a dazzling smile. "You have to admit,
Matty, I've got style."

"You've got gall is what you've got, Robert
Woodfynn."

They set off down the hill. They were near the bottom when Matty felt Moss peck gently at her ear. She
scanned the tall grass. Just above it two grouse were rising. Quickly she pushed up her sleeve and raised her

arm to the command position, curling her hand into a fist. Moss moved from Matty's shoulder and set down gently on the leather falconer's glove that sheathed her arm.

It was known throughout Barnsdale that Lord William, the best falconer in the region, passed his skills on to his daughter. Many said that Matty now surpassed him. The summer before, the villagers had even taken to calling her the Nut Brown Girl, for she roamed the countryside so constantly with her hawks that her skin had turned as dark as that of the peasants who tilled the fields. But Matty felt the truth in her bones. She would never be better than her father until she had reared a merlin. She had read what was known about the shrewd, stubborn birds in his spare book on falconry.

Thinking all this, Matty unleashed the jesses. A husky sound came from the back of her throat. *"Chahh!"*

Moss spread her wings and lifted off in flight.

Quickly the peregrine's wings became a blur as she skimmed after the grouse. The hawk anticipated their rate of ascent perfectly. Matty could almost feel Moss's muscles tighten for the kill. And then there was a flash as the peregrine went into a dive at a stupefying speed and snapped a grouse from the air. In a split second, drops of the grouse's blood flared against the pale sky. "Amazing!" Fynn whispered as Moss banked steeply to return with her catch.

The peregrine landed and dropped the bird at her mistress's feet. Matty crouched, speaking unintelligible words in a low, husky voice. Quickly severing the grouse's head, she put it in front of Moss, who puffed up her feathers greedily, stood on one leg, and then seized her prize. The rest Matty put in her cloth bag. Again she felt Fynn's eyes upon her.

Hubie Bigge had roused Fynn's temper the other day when he said that Matty was as good with a hawk as Fynn was with a bow. It pleased her as she recalled Hubie's praise. Was Fynn thinking about what Hubie had said now?

"Come on," Fynn said impatiently. "Let's join the boys. They'll be waiting."

"Ah, the feathered murderess and her accomplice have been at it again!" Will Scarloke said cheerfully as he spotted the bloody bag hanging from Matty's belt. The boys were at a large boulder near the creek where they were fishing.

"Don't call Moss that, Will. It's so rude," Matty said.

"Do you suppose, Matty," Will asked in the next breath, "that we could have a bit of down from Moss?"

"After you've called her a murderess! I wouldn't dare ask!"

"I agree with Matty," Rich Much said as he fiddled with his own fishing lure. "Very rude to insult her bird and then beg a feather." He pushed back his dark hair and squinted at the lure. "You know, this is very lovely, this lure—very elegant, I'd say, with this thistledown on it."

"Forget elegant! Will it catch fish?" Hubie Bigge asked. "I don't need feathers or dog hair. I got me own hair. It's red. It's wiry. It can't be beat for trout—better than mayflies or stone nymphs."

"I prefer a robin's feathers," Fynn said, "but hedgehog bristles serve well, too. Use them for fletching all my arrows and they works for fishing."

"That's the problem with your fishing, Fynn," Hubie said. "You think you're shooting an arrow and not casting a lure. It's not an attack."

"It's a deception," Will added with great authority.

Hubie scratched his head. His brow crinkled with sudden concern. "Hey, Fynn! Fish don't count, right?"

"Don't count for what?"

"Don't count as animals like harts and hinds. Your father and the other gamekeepers won't be on our tails, right?"

"Of course not. Are you daft? What do they care about a few trout?"

"I just wondered." Hubie glanced back over his shoulder slightly nervously. "Because when I was coming across the creek upstream, I swore I saw a man. But he jumped back in the shadows."

"Maybe he wasn't one of the gamekeepers but one of the king's forest officers," Rich said. "They know Fynn's father's been too soft with the locals. They're sending in some of the sheriff's men. At least that's what I've heard."

"But Fynn's father's gotten tougher," Will said. "Hauled in old Harry the cobbler. Found arrows in his house and a trap with harts' hair."

Fynn sighed. "Fishing isn't a problem. So don't worry about my father or the sheriff's men. They don't care about fishing." He fiddled with his lure, trying to attach some bristles to it.

But Matty understood Fynn and saw a shadow cross his face. He wasn't as unconcerned as he would like them to believe. She knew that he was not going to forget about the figure in the shadows. Fynn, of course, had the most to fear from being caught. His father might turn a blind eye, but the sheriff's forest officers would not.

The boys and Matty sat now under the budding branches of the tree near the creek, working diligently on their lures for the fish they knew would be rising as the day grew warmer. Matty carefully picked through the train of Moss's tail feathers and shook out a small clump of loose down. "Here you go, Will. This should do for more than one fishing lure."

"Yes, that will do," Will said. "Hubie, might you spare me some of your wiry hair for binding this?"

Hubert's face clenched as he pulled out a strand, then another, and another. In all he pulled out five.

Matty smiled. This was what she loved about being in the forest with her friends. They were all different but equal, and they shared everything, even hair! She wished it could be this way forever. She wished that they could always be here in the greenwood, smelling the wet bark on the trees, feeling the spongy moss that fleshed the earth and draped the rocks. In another few weeks the leaves would unfurl, casting lacy shadows and spreading an emerald light through the woods. It was early spring that Matty loved best with its promise of summer, more game, and more food. She knew she would give anything to freeze those moments in the dappled light of the greening forest.

Chapter 4

MATTY'S BRILLIANT IDEA

Frequent access to bathing water is essential for the health of a hawk's feathers. An ointment composed of equal parts crushed garlic, wormwood, and pine resin is serviceable for the common abrasions that hawks might suffer on their legs from chafing jesses.

HEN THEY NEXT MET, Hubie was bursting to tell them that he had seen the man again—the one he had glimpsed in the forest. Hubie called him the shadow man—and Will Scarloke suddenly exclaimed, "Treasure! He's burying treasure!"

The notion of treasure buried in the woods seized the boys. It made vague sense to Matty. Every week one heard of more nobles being robbed as well as treasures disappearing from churches and cathedrals. Catching the excitement, she thought, *Maybe someone will try to hide the Star of Jerusalem!*

"Near the creek," Hubie explained about the second sighting. "I thought I heard rustling when I came down to fish. I glimpsed someone, or I thought it was someone, but it was misty that day. It was like a dark shadow disappearing into a thicket. My first thought was that it was royal foresters. But there were none of the colors of the prince. It was just this sort of shape— black and gray. No heralds, no banners flying like they always have."

"Has it ever occurred to you that perhaps your stealing has caught up with you?" Matty asked. She looked directly at Fynn, for had he not recently brought down another deer?

"No!" all the boys chimed.

"They're not after petty thieves!" Rich said.

"And it's just one person, dressed all plain," Will added.

"The better to catch a poacher of the king's deer," Matty offered.

But the boys would hear none of it, and all began to speak. The air seemed to buzz with jeweled dreams and wisps of gold. Where would they dig first? They might all go off in different directions. Caves were always a sure bet for treasure. They must first check all the caves.

"Dig, yes, under large rocks," Will Scarloke decided.

"Stop! Stop!" Matty spoke loudly. "You are absolute fools. You're going to go digging holes all through these woods. How completely stupid! And what will Prince John's men or the sheriff's men think when they come riding through and their horses begin stumbling in these holes?"

"That someone's been digging for treasure," Hubie said enthusiastically, then suddenly realized the problem.

"Precisely." Matty nodded. Fynn lifted his chin slightly. He did not like the turn of events, even if Matty was right. He'd rather be wrong than bested by anyone. But the rest of the boys were now looking at Matty as if she possessed the wisdom of Solomon.

Matty knew exactly what they must do. They must be quiet and watchful like Ulysses the goshawk, perching high above the landscape and waiting, barely twitching a feather, ready to stoop at game rising from the brush. But of course in this case the "game" would not be "stooped," only watched.

"We should build a tree house," Matty said. A stillness descended upon the group. The boys' eyes sparkled with anticipation, for the next best thing to treasure would be to have a tree house. "We should have several tree houses, and camouflaged so that we can watch Prince John's men and the sheriff's men and perhaps glimpse this shadow man," Matty added. "But they cannot know."

"Brilliant!" Will exclaimed.

"Yes," Rich said. "Matty's idea is brilliant!"

"Well, it might work," Fynn said huffily. But he knew that it was a great plan, better than anything he could have thought up. Fynn felt like he'd been kicked in the stomach. He had to concede that all of them had been bested by a girl.

Chapter 5

FOUR TREE HOUSES

Like all living things hawks have their seasons. There are
times of yarak and times of molt. In times of yarak the
birds are keen and eager, and when molting they can be
cranky and dispirited. A good falconer is sensitive to the
hawk in all its moods, through all its seasons.

"No, Rich, not those hemlock boughs. They'll
stick out like a sore thumb with all this white."

Matty looked up from where she stood. In
this part of the forest there were entire groves of bright
white birch trees.

"Well, we're going to need more old man's beard,"
Rich said.

Old man's beard was a kind of gray and crinkly
moss that grew on the boulders near the creek.

The tree house in the birches was the fourth they had built in the last ten days. The plan had been to have five tree houses, one for each of them, strewn throughout the forest. In this way they could keep a close watch not just for treasure but on the royal foresters, too, if Prince John sent them.

The tree houses were lovely. Each one was made to blend with its surroundings. One had been constructed with a latticework of new green branches woven through with rushes and leaves. For another, in a sycamore that was unclimbable because of its bare trunk, they had designed a pulley system for raising and lowering a seat to where the branches began fifty feet above the forest floor. Then, high in an oak tree, they had woven a shelter made of vines and shredded bark that sat in the fork of two immense branches. In these leafy houses that seemed to float midst the trees, they wore tunics fashioned from bark strips and bleached reeds and helmets on their heads pieced together from broad leaves, so they, too, blended in perfectly. They could watch, yet never be seen. It had been Matty's idea that each tree house have its own set of clothes to disguise the watcher.

So now, as she went to gather some more old man's

beard, she remembered to take extra to tuck into their hair.

Of the houses they had been working on so far, this fourth one was Matty's favorite. It was like a twig cage covered almost completely with delicate green moss and silvery lichen. If she were to have a very fine dress, Matty thought, it would not be one sewn from beautiful silks with golden threads and French embroidery. Instead, she would have a skirt woven of moss and lichen. And rather than fine embroidery she would weave in woodland flowers like snow lilies, primroses, and bleeding heart. To Matty's mind that would be a dress fit for a queen.

As she approached the birch grove with her armload of moss, she saw that Will, Fynn, Rich, and Hubie stood in a tight cluster. She didn't know if it was the boys' posture or the way Will slowly turned his head toward her—not quite looking at her but still seeing her—that caused an immediate sense of alarm, alarm mixed with frustration.

Periodically the boys decided that she was not fit company. They always tried to be very kind as they patiently explained. "No, Matty, nothing personal. It's just that you're a girl."

This seemed very personal to Matty, and there was nothing she could do about it. Deep in her bones she knew that this was one of those moments.

"Matty," Fynn said. His brow was creased with concern, his voice gripped in tension. "We've seen the shadow man again." He paused. The other boys turned to watch her.

"So?" snapped Matty.

"So, we think it best that you not be about for a while." Fynn's square chin flinched and then he set his jaw firmly. Matty was furious. She had seen the set of that jaw before when Fynn made up his mind about something. She would not give up so easily.

"But that's the whole point—to see the shadow man or whoever it is. And there's still the other tree house to build. It was my 'brilliant' idea—remember!"

"Matty, it's simply too dangerous," Will Scarloke said. "For a girl, that is." He shifted his eyes quickly as he saw the fire in Matty's eyes.

"God's kneecaps, you are a pack of fools!" she hissed. Turning away from them, she plunged into the woods. She would build the fifth tree house herself. How could they stop her?

And she knew exactly where she would build it.

Near the creek, there was a stand of willows, one with spreading branches perfect for a tree house. She would make her walls of feathery willow branches and lace them together. It would not only be the prettiest of the tree houses but also the most concealed, for even after the willow leaves dropped, the thin whiplike branches would make a perfect screen.

She went to work immediately. It did not take her long to fix a small platform. The next step would be cutting the willow fronds from the trees by the creek. They were just this week unfurling their narrow, long leaves. She was not sure how long she had been working, but it was at least her fifth or sixth trip back from the creek banks with her armload of willow branches when she spotted Fynn near the base of the tree. He was wearing a new hat, more of a green hood, and looking up at the half-finished tree house.

"What are you doing here?" She let the bundle drop at her feet. He immediately ran over to pick it up. "I don't need your help, as you can well see."

"Yes, I can see that." Fynn stopped halfway as he bent down and looked up directly into her eyes.

What is this? she wondered. The incredible blueness of his eyes sometimes shocked her. They seemed set off by this new green hood that he had evidently fashioned out of a sleeve torn from his tunic with some leaves stuck into it. Did he know how blue his eyes were? She was furious with herself for even pondering such a stupid question. "How did you find me anyhow?"

"I track deer, remember?"

"I'm not a deer."

"I know. They can't build tree houses."

"Oh, thank you for the compliment. I'm overwhelmed."

"Yes, me, too," Fynn said, and glanced up at the tree house.

"What are you talking about?"

"I'm talking about how this is a better tree house, or it will be when it's finished, than any of ours."

"Am I supposed to thank you now?"

"Not yet."

Matty frowned and looked at him narrowly. "What do you mean, 'not yet'?"

"Well, I haven't apologized for my beastly behavior."

Matty was taken aback. She cocked her head and looked at him steadily. "Yes, you were a beast."

"Indeed, beastly, as I said."

"Well, I accept your apology for your utter beastliness."

"You had to say 'utter,' of course."

"Well . . . just beastliness then."

Fynn inhaled sharply. "Look, are we going to stand here and just toss the word *beastly* back and forth or what?"

"What do you mean by 'or what'?"

"I could help you with this, help you finish the tree house."

Matty opened her eyes wide with amazement. "Let you help *me* finish my own tree house! Oh, that's rare, truly rich, Fynn. You just told me I am building the best tree house of all. So I let you help me, and then you take the credit."

"I wouldn't take the credit. Never." His brow furrowed, and the bright blueness of his eyes suddenly seemed tarnished.

"Well, share it then. No! Fynn, I don't share. Not this!"

A dark ruddiness flushed Fynn's cheeks. He closed his eyes tight.

"What's wrong with you?" Matty asked.

He began to speak with his eyes still clamped

shut. "I'm telling myself not to get angry. I came to apologize."

Matty stepped closer to him and picked up his hand and squeezed it lightly. "And you did apologize and I thank you. But, Fynn, I just want to build my own tree house, that's all."

Chapter 6

STONE AND SHADOWS

Hawks are not known for being sociable creatures, but that does not mean they are untrainable.

THE FRAGILE BLUE OF the afternoon sky turned orange and then red as the sun sank until it broke like a bloodied yolk on the horizon. As twilight came, purple shadows like a bruise began to spread across the countryside and the Fitzwalter castle loomed dusky against the gathering clouds. The long, darker shadows of the turrets stretched across the barren field, reaching for her, or so it seemed to Matty. Something curled inside her, grew tight and cold as she approached her home. Were it not for the hawks and her father and Meg, there would be nothing to draw her to the castle. "Three years," Matty whispered to herself. Nearly three years had passed since that horrible day, and yet after two scouring winters one might still find bloodstains on the flagstones of the bailey. She always thought of this as she drew near the castle on her return from hunting.

For Matty, the castle represented a place of cold, dark stone that was the opposite from the world of the dense forests, the broad moors, meadows, and open fields she had come to know through falconry and with Fynn and his friends. Inside the castle there was nothing soft or yielding. Light, when it did finally pierce through the arrow-slit windows, fell like shards of glass on the granite. The shadows of the turrets lay like tombstones and seemed to press the very air with their weight.

Matty picked her way carefully across the drawbridge spanning the moat. It hadn't been lifted since the raid. The tower mews that had fallen victim to the catapult had never been rebuilt. The wreckage remained where it had fallen, for there were no servants or villeins left to repair or move it and her father and Hodge were much too old to carry rocks. This, in a sense, had been a blessing, for at Matty's suggestion a new mews had been improvised right in the keep, the strong central tower of the castle, where they now lived. Indeed the keep's topmost room, under the conical roof, was Matty's own chamber. Here, at least, the arrow-slit windows were in abundance, offering light and fresh air. It was almost as good as the old hawk house and in some ways better. She could be near the birds all the time. But as she walked through the bailey to the keep, she was struck by the loneliness of the castle. Before the raid her father had been a proud feudal lord, with over fifty men-at-arms and one hundred villeins, who lived and worked within the walls of the castle and its surrounding fields as part of their labor service to Lord William.

The Fitzwalters' castle had been full of life then. Walk into the bailey any time of the day or night and there was hustle and bustle, the banging of the blacksmith in his forge, the quacking of geese being marched toward a feeding trough by Meg. The boy who tended the kennels would run out to show Matty the first of a new litter of puppies. The cart of a villein loaded with the share of turnips and root vegetables due her father might have just pulled up at a storage cellar, and a dairymaid would be at the churn. But now they were all gone. Had it ever been real? Matty often wondered. It was as if it had been a play and all the actors had vanished from the stage.

Once Matty's family had lived throughout the

castle. But after the raid, as the hard times swept the land, servants left. Fires could not be kept burning in all the great fireplaces, and one by one the rooms of the castle had been closed. They seemed destined to live shrunken lives with only the dimmest memories of another time.

Matty looked up at the two other towers that jutted out from the castle and formed the main gatehouse, or barbican. There were no guards in the towers. Nor had there been since the raid, although she often thought about what a fat lot of good they had been. Her father suspected that they had been in the pay of the sheriff and had been the ones to sabotage the drawbridge. But who was really to blame? If the two ignorant tower guards had been bribed by the sheriff, were they at fault? No, in Matty's mind any blame rested firmly on the shoulders of Prince John. Prince John with his dreams of conquest that were nothing like his brother Richard's dreams of conquering the Holy Land for Christians. Now that old King Henry had died, John wanted to conquer England for himself.

Everyone in the shire, be they noble or peasant, was teetering on the edge of starvation. Matty had to go out every day to hunt as the pottage simmering on the fire grew thinner and thinner with more water and less meat. Matty had found a worm in her trencher from a rotten potato thrown into the thin stew. The worm had crept out and been boiled.

"Meg," Matty called as she came into the keep, "I brought a duck. It's not much."

"Don't worry, dear. We'll make do." Matty's old nursemaid took the duck and with her other hand, touched Matty's cheek. "Thank you, child."

"No rabbits yet, eh, Matilda?" Lord William's voice came out of a shadowy corner where he was mending some jesses for the hawks.

"None in the snare, Father."

He sighed, then tried to sound more hopeful. "Well, another two weeks, they'll be plentiful and you can bet that Ulysses will give them a run for it. Moss, too, for that matter."

"Yes. Soon the rabbits will be scampering," Matty replied. There was a clinking sound from another corner. On a stool Hodge worked on a hauberk, a chain mail shirt. Hodge had awakened one morning that winter not recognizing his own wife. The years of marriage had somehow been forgotten. He thought he was once more preparing his master, Lord William, for battle on the French fields under the command of young Prince Richard. Since that morning, Hodge had spent endless hours mending and re-mending the same sleeve.

Matty's eyes slid toward the old man. He seemed a symbol of everything that had been lost, perhaps most of all lost hope. Why should she believe that things would change for him, for any of them? It could only get worse, especially when winter set in again. But it was not yet spring. Why was she already anticipating winter? Only the most desperate thought of winter on the brink of spring.

Matty helped Meg prepare the paltry meal. The one good thing about so little to eat was that one did not linger at the table. There were no dishes to wash since they began using the bread trenchers. One just wiped them and kept using them until they fell apart.

"May I be excused?"

"Yes," Lord William said, "but first tell me about the hawking. How did Moss fly?"

Meg and Lord William both looked at her. Their eyes had a dim light, like the guttering flicker of a candle. *Give us something . . . give us any shred of hope.* It was not simply hawking they wished to know about.

"No news of King Richard?" her father whispered as if the very words might shatter.

Much had changed and yet not enough. After Richard had returned from France to receive his crown in the autumn of the year 1189, peace had somehow been brokered with his brother Prince John. William Longchamp, the Bishop of Ely, confidant of Richard and priest to his mother, Queen Eleanor, had been appointed the chancellor. He was the most important official next to the king, and hopes for change and prosperity were high. But within a scant two months of Richard's return came of the fall of Jerusalem to the Saracen leader Saladin. The king had hardly settled in before he left for the Third Crusade to the Holy Land, and Prince John had become more ruthless than ever.

Meg and her father strained for hope.

"No rumors?" Meg asked. "You didn't pick up any rumor when you be out hunting?"

Matty was tempted to say that hunting was not like going to town and that ducks and rabbits don't exactly speak. She merely shook her head. "Sorry," she said softly. "Haven't heard a thing." She got up to leave. "Maybe . . ." but the words dwindled off and no one was looking at her now.

Chapter 7

ANSWERED PRAYERS

Merlins are falcons, members of the long-winged hawk family, as opposed to the "true hawks" or short-winged hawks. In the beginning stages of their education they can be fitful and stubborn. Despite this temperament once the falconer has gained the trust of a merlin, that trust is unparalleled within the kingdom of hawks.

THE NEXT DAY FYNN came by to fetch Matty just as dawn broke. They were on their way to meet the boys. They had not gone far when Fynn found the droppings of a large deer and became determined to track it. Matty followed him with growing impatience, and, after almost half an hour when no deer could be spotted and the track had more or less dissolved into nothingness, Matty went up and tugged on his sleeve.

"Fynn, let's go. The deer must have disappeared. Come on," Matty urged, but Fynn walked on stubbornly. "Fynn, can't you put down that bow for a moment? Besides, you know there've been royal foresters spotted around here."

"My pa says they only come by once or twice a month."

"Let's meet the boys."

"Not yet. If I can't get this deer, I'll get something else with my bow." To taunt her, he added, "I don't have to wait on a falcon."

"Falconry, Robert Woodfynn, is an *art* as well as a method of gathering food."

"So is hunting, Matilda Fitzwalter."

"No, not really. It has no subtlety."

"Don't use big words. Just because you can read and write better than any of us doesn't give you the right to use big words."

"All right. Archery is a crude form of hunting. You don't have to feed a bow, care for it, and learn its ways."

"That just proves how little you know about wood, Mistress Matilda."

"Don't call me Mistress Matilda. I don't like it."

"Oh, don't get your breeches in a twist."

"What?" Matty exclaimed. "Since when do girls wear breeches? I thought you knew better than that, Robin Woodfynn!"

"Well, your whatevers," he replied, blushing to the root of every hair on his head.

Now, as Matty walked through the meadow grass, she stopped suddenly. Just ahead in the heather she thought she caught a flash of white. There was a sudden blurring, then a speck of gold, as if a tiny piece of the sun had tumbled down to earth.

Matty began to creep quietly up to the clump of heather. *Something's caught!* In the next moment she heard a frantic beating, followed by a series of weak calls that sounded like *eep-eep-eep*. There was something in the thin sound that made Matty guess that it was a food call of some sort. When she was nearly upon the heather, she looked down and gasped. She was staring at the dark-brown feathers of a merlin, a newly fledged merlin! And each time it blinked, there was a tiny flash of gold in its dark eyes.

Matty could tell that the merlin was in poor

condition. She judged it to be a female by its color. Every time the bird beat her wings Matty could glimpse the lighter brown-and-white speckles of its breast and underwings. But there were hunger streaks too. The *eep-eep* vocalizations had definitely been desperate calls for food. The merlin had become ensnared in the remnants of netting from a trap of some sort, but it also had the shreds of jesses on one leg. Matty realized that this bird was exactly what her father had described—a frustrated falconer's castoff. But so soon? she wondered. It seemed, even with the hunger streaks, to have recently grown feathers.

The bird went into a complete panic as it looked up at Matty, giving a loud *ki-ki ka-ka* cry of alarm. Matty had to think fast. Looking at the bird, she saw a bedraggled, starving creature but she also saw something more. The tiny flash of gold in the dark eyes again! "Marigold," she whispered. This merlin *had* to live. Her father had said that to truly become a great falconer one needed a merlin. This bird could become the means of achieving all her deepest hopes. Their destinies just maybe were intertwined.

Taking the hem of her dress and giving a quick glance around for Fynn, she began to tear it apart.

But the fabric was tough homespun. "No, no, this is not working," she muttered. Then quickly, she lifted her skirts and pulled off her underskirts. Made of a softer material, they easily ripped. She had to hood this bird, and if it had to be with her garments so be it! Hooding the bird was the only way to calm her, and once calmed, she would be named! Yes, Matty would croon this name, *Marigold*, softly to the young bird until she recognized it as her own.

On her first attempt all she got was an angry stab in the palm of her hand. Weak as the merlin was, it was not afraid. It was angry and ready to attack.

Matty finally succeeded in twisting a scrap of cloth around the young hawk's head. She would have to leave the mesh tangled around the bird's foot for now.

She began to take the merlin to the castle, whispering softly.

"Whatcha got there, Matty?" Fynn said, coming up to her and looking down at the bundle in her hands with the mesh trailing from it. The merlin had calmed down quite a bit, but at the sound of a new voice she began to bate and flutter.

"Sssh!" Matty said.

"But what is it?"

"Can't you tell, Fynn?"

"Come on. Whatcha got?"

"So you really want to know?"

"Yes, Matty, I really want to know."

"It's my—whatevers—in a twist!" She smiled slyly. Then both Matty and Fynn blushed madly. For indeed Fynn was staring straight at these most intimate of feminine garments and Matty had dared to joke about it.

Then Fynn reached out and tucked a dark curl that had escaped from behind her ear. He left his hand behind her ear for a moment too long.

"I've got to be getting on," she said, and dipped her chin so he could not see the confusion in her eyes.

When she had walked on several paces and finally collected herself, she turned back and gave him a dazzling smile. "I found a merlin. They say they are the cleverest and the most ambitious of birds. Some say the noblest of all hawks."

"Well, then this bird has met its match for a mistress, I daresay!" Fynn replied, his voice suddenly husky. Matty felt her heart race. She shut her eyes for a second and then continued walking.

Chapter 8

THE LIGHT BEHIND THE SHADOW

A babe might have a wet nurse, but a nobleman who keeps a hawk master shall fail. There is no joy in taking a hawk taught on another person's fist.

As MATTY MOUNTED THE stairs after a day's hunting with Lyra, she could hear the hawks in the mews. Their muted caws and chirps, their talons making little scratching noises on their perches was a wonderful music: it dispelled the darkness of the stone and lightened the shadows of the castle.

The moment she passed through the doorway she felt calm. This was the only place she was really at home. The room itself was large and circular. Several perches radiated from notches in the stone wall like the spokes of a wheel. Lyra returned to her perch closest to one of the windows. Beside her perched the kestrel Morgana. Next to her was Ulysses, then Moss, and finally Marigold.

The walls of the circular chamber were divided into three sections. The birds occupied the largest section that went halfway around the tower. The two remaining sections were almost equal in size. The first was lined with benches on which an assortment of hawking equipment had been neatly laid—leashes; boxes with imping needles; waxed thread; a few pots filled with ointments, powders, and oils; small knives; and a stone slab on which to cut up tiny morsels of mouse or whatever meat was on the day's menu. Sometimes she was lucky and caught a small rat in one of her traps. At one end of the benches there were two huge basins for bathing the birds. One was filled with water, the other with sand for dust baths in cold weather. Above the benches were neat rows of pegs from which hung several jesses and other equipment. Then above these pegs was a shelf for the tiny, beautiful leather hoods. Some of these hoods were quite old, going back scores of years. All were painted in the Fitzwalter colors of crimson and green. The third section was Matty's own space: a bed shoved into a wall niche, a few pegs, and a basin for slops.

Twenty feet above, under the cone of the turret's roof, Fynn had helped Matty hoist a platform that supported cages on its cross arms. It was a perfect loft space for molting birds. When raptors molt, they become finicky and sometimes cantankerous. It was best for them to be separated from the other hawks at such times.

Matty kept the tower room immaculate. On the floor beneath the birds' perches was a thick layer of sawdust and wood shavings from the days when the castle had employed a sawyer to cut their firewood. Mattie covered this layer with rushes, strewed it with dried herbs—sage, chamomile, hyssop, and balm—and changed it often. She scraped the perches regularly and swept the chamber daily, scrubbing the stones weekly. The birds themselves were groomed and trimmed and clipped; their beaks and talons coped, or filed and snipped. When the shaft of one of their feathers was bent, Matty straightened it by pressing it with cloths soaked in hot water. If it was broken off, she had her supply of molted feathers carefully arranged in the special box. To Matty the world within the tower mews was as perfect a place as one could be if not outside hunting with the hawks or in the forest of Barnsdale with Fynn and the boys. It was a place of order, where living things were cared for and respected. It was the kind of world, Matty thought, that Richard could make if he would return as king.

It had been more than two weeks since she had brought Marigold back to the castle. And for those two weeks Matty had spent nearly every hour with her, only leaving to hunt for food. She sensed that Lyra and Morgana were a bit jealous of her attention to the little merlin. Ulysses was a bird of extreme patience and maturity. He and Moss seemed to understand completely what it took to raise a young hawk. Moss knew better than any of them what was required to teach a young one, for she had taught Matty. Her devotion was ardent, almost maternal, and what was dear to Matty was unquestionably dear to Moss.

When Matty had found Marigold in the meadow, she was not even sure the merlin would survive. The young bird needed loving attention. Hunger, already shown by the streaks in her plumage, threatened to weaken every important flight feather in Marigold's body.

If the young merlin had been previously trained, it counted for nothing. Matty had to begin all over again—hooding her, carrying her practically every available waking moment, talking constantly so that Marigold would know her voice. Matty tried to feed the merlin freshly caught mice, but feeding a merlin was not a simple matter. Her father had explained that a merlin's diet had to be carefully monitored in relation to its growth because of the bird's active nature and its rapid heartbeat. To calculate the growth, it was necessary to measure the bird's wings each day and then weigh the food. Within the two weeks since she had found Marigold, Matty's skill in mathematics had leaped forward.

But this merlin challenged her at every opportunity, and it was lucky that Matty lived in the tower mews so that she could be with Marigold all night, as was required in these first critical weeks of her training. During those long vigils as the moon rose and set, Matty often thought of that odd conversation she had with Fynn on the day she found the merlin. There had been her bold banter, which now hardly seemed all that bold. But then Fynn had touched her, tucked the lock of hair behind her ear. That moment she played and replayed in her head. The memory sent shivers through her. She could not recall the words, but she could almost hear the tone of his voice. It was different; it wasn't that I'm-so-clever tone. Not a trace of raillery or ribbing. Fynn had sounded, for one of the few times in his life, very serious. They had both, she guessed, grown in more ways than one.

Matty was now twelve and a half years old. In the years since the raid the birds, too, had matured. They recognized her voice and the way she breathed. A mysterious link had been forged between the girl and the birds, an intimacy and trust beyond what most falconers could imagine.

Marigold was already beginning to bond with Matty. And though the merlin was still far from tamed, a mutual respect had grown between them. By the third week of her training, Marigold had stopped her bating, or temper tantrums, during which she would leap from Matty's fist in headlong dives of rage and defiance.

Now Matty cooed and sang as she softly approached her merlin. "Marigold," she whispered. "Marigold!" Ah! The small hooded head turned toward her, and the bird rustled her feathers. She lifted her foot as she heard Matty pull on the leather glove. Marigold was ready, eager to step on to Matty's arm. This was a very good sign.

Matty could hear Morgana and Lyra grumbling softly. Even though Lyra had just been out with her and Morgana the day before, they were still greedy for attention. She knew exactly what they were saying: *Never even looks at us, does she?*

She heard Moss trying to soothe their obviously ruffled feathers with patience and reason. *"Ku lu pshaw gru gru."* (This is important. A delicate point in the merlin's training.) Matty nodded appreciatively. Then Ulysses came in with a harsh scolding to Lyra and Morgan. *"Ki ki kak ki kak. . . ."* (You know nothing of training or discipline. You forget your own days when Lord William spent hundreds of hours with you. Be a little more gracious, you slovenly ingrates!) The two birds were instantly chastened and settled down.

Matty continued with the merlin. She had learned most of the important vocalizations needed to communicate with the bird, especially the soothing ones that could calm her. *"Ptschaw, chu chu,* nice girl me, Marigold. *Cha ka? Chu sho mwap.* No, no . . . that's a sweet *tsha,"* she whispered.

The merlin climbed onto her fist and then her arm. Matty, her lips nearly touching the hood, kept speaking softly in an odd mixture of English and the sounds that she sensed were peculiar to merlins and then the others that she generally used to speak with her birds. These sounds came burbling up from the back of her throat, whispering over her tongue with a velvety softness. Marigold was listening. Matty could tell that she was understanding more and more. Perhaps tonight Matty would remove her hood.

A hawk must be unhooded for the first time in nearly complete darkness. One could never be too careful when first releasing a bird from the hood into the light. The time must be well chosen and the light well placed. So Matty would begin at midnight. In the meantime she would carry the little merlin with her as she tidied the chamber and tended the other birds.

For long hours a curved sliver of the moon moved across the sky until now it was setting and the mews grew darker. Matty sensed the moment approaching even as she slept with her arm propped on a small crutch, the merlin perched on her glove. Almost immediately she was awake and alert. She transferred Marigold to a special low perch near her bed and fetched a candle. She put the candle as far from the merlin as possible, then lit it. She went back and placed Marigold on her fist.

"*Ptschaw, mwap, chu chu.* Nice Marigold. *Chu sho no no* . . . that's a sweet *tsha. Cha ka. Hschaw sachwa,* my Marigold."

Matty began to carefully loosen the braces at the back of Marigold's hood. She'd chosen it carefully. The gilt initials WF, once bright as the gold in Marigold's eyes, were now dim, the leather supple with age. One quick tug slackened the braces entirely and the hood slipped a bit. The merlin remained calm. Matty took hold of the plume on the hood and pulled gently. The hood was off! Marigold immediately swung her tiny head toward the pool of honey-gold light cast by the candle. "*Tschaw ptschaw lucca lucca*. Yes, Marigold, yes, dear, a bit of candlelight." The most exciting part of the entire taming and teaching period was about to happen.

Soon Matty would turn her own head slowly toward the merlin and look deeply into Marigold's eyes. This was when Matty would discover if she and the hawk had a true connection, an inviolable bond. What Matty saw in those eyes would influence the rest of the merlin's education. She felt her own heart beat faster. The bird shifted on her fist as if she sensed her mistress's quickening pulse. Now Matty bent her head very close. She whispered softly. "*Ptschaw chatau,* my Marigold."

Until Matty received a signal, she would not look directly in the merlin's eyes. So Matty kept her head turned slightly away. After a barely discernible ruffling of Marigold's feathers, ever so slowly Matty began to turn her head, her eyes cast down. All the while she stroked Marigold's talons, her wing edges, and her brown breast with its flecks of gray and purple. And now Matty felt it. The gold slivers, like tiny arrows lighting up her face. She was caught in the merlin's gaze. Matty looked up. Her eyes were met by others as curious as her own. Not shy but trusting, intelligent, and ready for more. In the candlelight the bird and the girl peered at each other. It was as if two lost friends had finally met.

Chapter 9

FIRST FLIGHT

There is that moment for every falconer that is the most difficult when the jesses are released and the hawk is first tried. Will the hours, the weeks, the months result in not simply a bird ready to hunt but a bird with whom a trust has been built? The bird will fly off for the prey, but the real question is will it return to its master?

"*Chwap chawap ptutch.*" (Lark wings delicious.) Two days after Marigold's unhooding, Matty stood in the middle of the bailey in front of the old mews. She held a length of cord to which a pair of bloody lark wings was attached. As Matty swung the lure, she cajoled and encouraged Marigold, who was tethered on a creance, or training line, several yards away. She wanted the merlin to fly to the lure. "*Phryn, darm*. You are a lovely, strong merlin. You will be a wonderful hunter."

Matty watched Marigold carefully. She saw the dark eyes with the tiny gold flecks tracking the swing of the lure. The merlin roused her wings and made a quick, low-skimming flight, striking the lure with her talons.

From the window high in the keep Lord William observed this scene and marveled at his daughter. Her skills were unbelievable. A merlin, no less, and she had the bird flying to the lure faster than he had ever taught any hawk to do anything. But it was not just her obvious talent for communication. She had fed this bird perfectly. Every bird needed a little bit of fat. Figuring out a bird's ideal weight was difficult. Too light and without enough fat the bird could appear quite healthy but might not have the energy to hunt successfully.

The late afternoon shadows stretched across the bailey, but Matty and her bird seemed to sparkle even in the dwindling light of the day. "She's ready, Matty!" Lord William called down. "She's ready!"

Matty tipped her head up. "You really think so, Father?"

"I know so!" Lord William exclaimed.

* * *

With any luck the larks would be out today, Matty thought as she walked toward the meadow with Marigold on her shoulder. It was dry and sunny. The warm columns of air would be rising, making the wonderful updrafts that birds loved, for they could soar and hardly needed to flicker a wing for a good ride. She was excited and she hoped she didn't run into Fynn or Rich and the others. She did not want any spectators around for Marigold's first free flight. The bird was beautiful now. Her plumage was an amazing rich brown, and if one looked closely one could detect dark purple undertones, the color of summer plums.

Matty's first instincts about Marigold had been right. This merlin was going to be a hawk among hawks, a hawk for kings and emperors. But Marigold was *her* merlin.

Matty felt the puff and shiver of the little hawk on her shoulder as soon as they approached the meadow. It was a sign of excitement. Although no larks were immediately visible, Marigold must have sensed them nearby. Then one darted out of a hedge and three more followed.

At the first sight of the larks, the taste of bloody

wings flooded through the bird's crop, the sac deep in a bird's throat where its prey is first digested. "*Hulla hulla mwatch . . . Chwap chawap ptutch.*" Matty spoke softly while she loosened the jesses. The words like small burrs caught in the air between them as she moved her mouth to within inches of Marigold's beak.

"Sweet *tsha. Ptschaw chu chu,* beauty Marigold. *Cha ka? Chu sho mwap. Mrrru shru cha ptschaw.*"

The leashes were off. Matty knelt on the ground, for she wanted Marigold to take off low, which would give her a long horizontal flight and time to discover for herself that she was truly free in the outdoors. Matty raised her arm and gave the command. Without a moment's hesitation Marigold lifted off, at first skimming the ground and then rising in an aggressive flight to track the singing larks. Matty waited with her hands clasped at her breast. She could feel her heart beating through the stiff leather of the falconer's glove. She could almost feel the thrill of the bird's own beating heart. Marigold had not looked back. She was drunk with freedom. Matty watched as Marigold caught the changing angle of the breeze that curled around the treetops. The larks sensed her presence even though she flew high above them. Nervously twittering, they made desperate dashes against a sudden headwind. Just as the fattest of the birds was right over the middle of the field, Matty saw Marigold begin to plunge toward the earth. Her legs flattened backward against her half-closed tail; her wings folded close to her sides; the sharp little beak cut the air. She hurled down like a dart. There was a spray of feathers, then a splattering of blood. It had all happened so fast that it took Matty a moment to catch her breath.

Next she wondered what every falconer wondered on the occasion of a bird's first free flight. Would the merlin—besotted with freedom—fly away forever? Would Marigold return when Matty whistled? Or would she lose her?

But Marigold did return. The little hawk had hardly settled back on Matty's shoulder when a shiver ran up Matty's spine. Someone was watching her. She felt strange eyes drilling into her back, but she dared not turn around to look. Fear flooded her. *Would that I were a bird and could fly from this earth!* Was this an idle wish? It seemed to Matty as if she had suddenly struck upon a truth at the core of her being.

Finally, her fear lessened. She felt she had been released from the staring eyes that had locked on her. But she waited. Marigold sensed her mistress's caution. She cocked her head, to pick up any sounds. Matty listened, too. She knew the natural noises of the forest. The tread of a deer was different from that of a fawn. The owl flew sheathed in silence, but the wind curled off the edges of a hawk's wings in a muffled roar. Matty crouched near the trunk of a gnarled oak tree with Marigold on her shoulder and listened for the sound of human footsteps. But finally, when all felt quiet, Matty stood up and began the long walk back to the castle.

That evening after Matty returned to the mews, she felt a mixture of joy and apprehension. Someone had been spying on her, she was sure. She could not shake the shreds of that fear that had so suddenly invaded her entire being. Sleep was hard to come by as the moon, now broad as a curved blade, rose in the night. Matty felt her eyelids grow heavy. But in the last few months—particularly in the weeks since she had found Marigold and all the hours she had to stay with her when normal sleep had been impossible— she was aware that it was not exactly in sleep that she sometimes experienced a kind of rest that was more like a waking dream, a trance.

Tonight Matty was very much aware of being in this peculiar condition. Perhaps she had been in this state since Marigold's flight that afternoon. She opened her eyes wide and seemed to find herself at a slight remove from her own body as if she were on a perch. She felt an odd stirring in her shoulders, and when she looked down she could see a tiny ant crawling in a crack in the floor. She blinked and looked around, seeing not just a spider in its web but the tiny hairs on each of its eight legs. Her eyes had never seen with such sharpness, such astounding clarity. And suddenly she sensed that her arms no longer felt like arms. What was happening? She was out of her own body but not quite in another. She felt part girl but part not girl. She experienced a faint pull in her head, as if she were being drawn elsewhere. *Am I becoming a hawk?* But the instant the thought occurred to her she was back in her own bed. She was not frightened in the least . . . perhaps a bit wistful. For there was a sense of loss for what had just vanished.

Chapter 10

THE PRIORY AT BARNSDALE

For a true falconer a well-taught bird is never a captive but a partner.

I T WAS SUNDAY MORNING and Matty was sitting by her father in the pew of the chapel of the priory of Barnsdale when she felt a ping on the back of her neck. She knew immediately what it was even before she saw the little needle of thistle land on her shoulder. Fynn must be sitting behind her. He was almost as good a shot with a thistle and a hollow reed to blow through as he was with a bow and arrow. Matty turned around. She was struck suddenly by how tall he appeared—even sitting in the pew—and how broad his shoulders had become. There were even the first signs of a mustache! They had never spoken of that day when Matty had found Marigold and Fynn had declared the merlin a match for its mistress. She had never forgotten his expression and the play of light in his eyes when he had spoken those words. She counted back and realized that she had known Fynn for nearly half her life. She was thirteen now and he was well past fourteen but still acted like a mischievous boy. Well, she was hardly a lady herself.

Another thistle leaf hit the back of her neck. She turned again to look at her assailant. Fynn attempted to suppress a smile and maintain a solemn look, but his eyes sparkled with sly humor. He nodded toward the aisle. She cautiously slid her gaze to the side. Hubie was actually tying a fishing fly in church. If this wasn't sacrilegious she didn't know what was. But it made Matty laugh. Luckily the nuns had just begun the loudest part of their hymn, the part that led up to the Eucharist. Father Percival was getting ready to lift the holy bread. This was the moment when the Real Presence of Lord Jesus was to be recognized. *Fly tying at a moment like this!* Matty bit the insides of her mouth to keep from laughing aloud and prayed not to burst out into a storm of giggles. Was that a horrible thing to pray for? Thank heavens the nuns were trilling loudly and Father Percival was chanting in a thunderous voice. There was enough noise for some cover. But Hubie! So cocky, so pleased with himself. She looked again, and Will gave her the signal to wait after church.

Between Hubie's fly tying, Will's signal, and two more thistle leaves blown on her neck by Fynn, there was precious little time to concentrate on the service or the other people in the church. Several of the sheriff's men were present as were some richly clad gentlemen who could only be courtiers of the prince.

Standing next to the old abbess from the nearby Abbey of St. Michael was a younger woman who also wore an abbess's cross. Matty kept looking back at her. She was large with a heavy brow. There was something odd about her eyes—they were the kind of eyes that could pierce you. Matty shivered. They reminded her of something. She was not sure what, but she did not want this woman looking at her. She sank down a bit in the pew but tried to swivel her head and slide her eyes over for another glance.

In the shadow of the larger woman, the older abbess seemed to have shrunk and withered since last Sunday. What was happening? And who was this large lady?

What was it about her eyes that so disturbed Matty? Was it like trying to stare into the sun? But they were not bright. The eyes seemed colorless, empty. And yet they had a power. Matty did not want to look at them, but she was drawn, as one might be drawn to the edge of a cliff, to peer into a deep chasm. Matty finally tore her eyes away and shook her head. She felt an overwhelming sense of threat. She wanted to get out of the church. Would the services never end? Father Percival could drag out a prayer longer than any person she knew.

Finally Matty heard the words of the benediction and the church service concluded. As she left, she brushed by the young abbess but kept her head down as if studying the stone pattern of the floor with great intensity. Outside, Fynn was looking about furtively. "What is it?" Matty said, coming up to the boys.

"The sheriff's men are gone," Will said. "They don't like church much more than we do."

"We have to meet this evening, dusk. The big rock by the creek," Fynn said. "Now scatter. We can't be seen together."

Chapter 11

THE EYES

Like all wild things hawks can smell fear. Therefore, it is best when dealing with birds of prey to keep one's wits and stay calm. In this way a hawk will come to you.

"IT WAS HER EYES." Matty looked around the circle of boys.

"What do you mean, her eyes?" Fynn leaned forward on the staff he had made from a limb of an alder.

"Fynn, they were transparent!"

"Transparent!" Will exclaimed. "How can eyes be transparent?"

"Hers were, I tell you, and it was the most terrible thing I ever saw." Matty paused. "It was as if . . ." She hesitated, groping for the right words as she tried to remember the terrible cold feeling that had crept through her when she had seen the abbess. "It was as if they looked not just through you, but you could see through them and into her. And there . . . there was nothing . . . nothing human—nothing living inside! Yes, that's it. It was as if those eyes belonged to nothing human or living on earth. They were eyes from the realm of the dead." She looked directly at the boys, who drew in closer as she spoke. "And they reminded me of something. I can't explain, but I felt they had seen me before."

"The eyes had seen you before?" Rich asked, confused. "Are you trying to say she recognized you or you recognized her?"

"I—I . . ." Matty shook her head. "I don't know. It just all felt very queer to me."

"So you think," Rich continued, "that she could be taking over from the old abbess?"

"No," Fynn said. "I heard my father say that there is a new abbess at the big abbey in Nottingham and that's just my point, lads."

"What's the point?" Matty said.

"It's why Hubie called the meeting, isn't it, Hubie?"

"Well, yes, but—" Hubie started to speak then Rich interrupted.

"Oh, this is the missing chalice thing," Rich said.

"The missing chalice thing!" Fynn mimicked with undisguised contempt. "It's real, Rich. Don't make fun of it."

"My mum noticed it was gone. But she wasn't sure of its value," Hubie offered.

"I noticed it was gone, too. Since three Sundays ago, right?" Matty said.

"Are you talking about the chalice with the rubies?" Will interrupted.

"Exactly," Fynn said. "It hasn't been there in its niche for these past three Sundays!"

"So what's the point?" asked Rich.

"The point is this," Fynn said more quietly. "Prince John has King Richard just where he wants him—miles away. Right now Prince John is the most powerful man in England and pretty near the richest. But there is still also one powerful man who stands in his way and has remained loyal to King Richard."

"Who's that?" Rich asked with sudden respect.

Matty watched Fynn carefully. He could certainly command attention when he wanted to. There was a force to the way he spoke. In a mews there was always one hawk who emerged as the leader. In hers it was old Moss whom the others, even the arrogant Morgana, regarded highly. Fynn was definitely the leader here. He did not have to be called that. He simply was.

"Go on, Fynn," Matty said softly. He cast her a quick glance. "Who is it?"

"The Bishop of Ely, William Longchamp. He is the only high churchman who has been honest, faithful to his king and his flock. And he is the chancellor. That means that he is supposed to be the boss while Richard is away. He's meant to keep an eye on Prince John, I'll wager."

"But what does this have to do with the church, except that he is a bishop?" Will asked.

Fynn lowered his voice to a whisper. "The church is rich. John has drained the nobles of every penny. On top of that, there are these new taxes for the Crusades. Now you watch, Prince John will turn more and more to the church. Its treasures could raise him an army. I'll wager the Bishop of Ely is going to make it more difficult for him to get what he wants. Probably already has."

"But the Bishop of Ely is far from here and from

this church. I'm sure he doesn't know that the chalice has gone missing," Rich said.

"But there are rumors about another bishop, a bad one who is closer to here, to Barnsdale—the Bishop of Hereford," said Hubie. "He's Prince John's supporter."

"And," Will added, "he works closely with Prince John's chief bully, Sir Guy of Gisborne."

Matty turned pale at the mere mention of Sir Guy. The memory of him standing in the bailey holding up her mother's necklace with its Star of Jerusalem sapphire dripping blood was still vivid in her mind's eye.

"You all right, Matty?" Fynn asked with sudden concern. She blinked rapidly and shook her head as if to banish the horrible image. "I wonder sometimes," she said slowly, "whatever happened to my mother's necklace." The boys looked at one another.

"What necklace?" Will asked.

"A necklace my father gave her at the time of my birth. It held a blue star sapphire called the Star of Jerusalem. Very rare. She wore it as a pendant."

"Well, if Gisborne has it, I'm sure he's holding it for Prince John. A bargaining chip to buy loyalty," Rich said.

"Prince John," Fynn continued, "needs many for his plans—traitors, schemers, varlets—all kinds. Not just the sheriff and Gisborne. Like Hubie said, he's got the Bishop of Hereford, as corrupt a man as any. And I'll bet you the abbess is connected to *him*."

Rich stood up suddenly. He was an astute lad with a sense of political maneuverings. On first glance, Rich looked as plain as a potato. His hair was a dusty brown and tiny freckles were scattered across his cheeks. His eyes were a very ordinary gray until he got an idea. Then they sparkled. "That makes sense. I heard, too, that there was a new abbess in the Nottingham abbey. How convenient for her to work with the sheriff. And the sheriff is owned by Prince John, who wants to own the church. Oh, yes, it all begins to fit neatly, doesn't it? A devilish design of scoundrels and tyrants and rotten men of the cloth!"

"And women," Matty said softly. "It's like a giant chess game, isn't it? Bishop against bishop, knights and rooks for the prince—like Gisborne and the sheriff. The king virtually checkmated in the Holy Land. And all of us are the pawns, of course."

There was a deep silence. Then Rich said, "But there's more to this—this . . ." He hesitated.

"This game," Fynn said.

"More?" Hubie said. His large round face was flushed, and an anxious look clouded his green eyes.

"Yes." Fynn began to pace in front of the rock where they had gathered. "My father was saying last night that more forest land—it's not only Barnsdale but also Sherwood Forest—has now been forbidden to hunters, save for the prince's and the sheriff's men."

Hubie sighed. "There's not going to be a thing to be had to eat if on top of all these taxes people can't hunt anywhere. I don't know what my mum's going to do. When I deliver to the alehouses, I have to pay the gate tax. It's doubled in the past year. It really cuts into our profits."

"The millers' taxes have gone up, too," Rich said. "The customs officers used to come once a year, but now they come every four months. They think we're so stupid. They say they are charging us less, but I said to me da, 'Tell them we can multiply, Da. If they be charging us one pound three times a year, that is three pounds instead of the two pounds once a year we used to pay, plus the four bags of milled grain they now add.'"

"What did your da say?" Matty asked.

"He said, 'Don't question, don't argue. We don't want trouble from them.'"

"You see," Fynn continued, "every time you turn around, they are claiming more, be it land or taxes, in the name of the king. But we know John isn't claiming it for King Richard. And now that the people have been bled, he turns to the church. Can't tax the church, but why not steal from it?" Fynn paused and let that sink in.

"So what are we to do?" Matty asked.

"I'm not sure," Fynn said, "but the chalice is gone. It must be somewhere."

Exactly a week later, when the boys and Matty took their places in church, the chalice was back in its niche. Matty noticed it first and nudged Hubie, who was on his knees beside her praying. He opened his eyes wide, then blinked, then nudged Fynn, who blew a thistle leaf through a reed at Rich. Rich turned around and mouthed, "Unbelievable!"

Chapter 12

FIFTH TREE HOUSE

A hunting bird that attempts to fly off the fist before its jesses are loosened should never be helped back on. It must learn to pull itself up on its own.

IT WAS MONDAY, THE day after the mysterious reappearance of the chalice. It had disturbed them all, of course, for without theft there could be no thieves. Rich declared that it most likely had been taken to a silversmith for repair. Matty reflected on all this as she sat in her tree house, the one she had built by herself. The long slender branches of the willow hung like a veil against the day. She peered out through the lovely strands of ivy that she had woven into the tendrils of willow. She often came to the tree house to think, bringing her birds, for it was quiet and afforded a good vantage point for spotting game.

On this day she had brought Moss along with Ulysses and Marigold. Moss fascinated Matty. The peregrine had aged significantly, and she was now nearly blind. Matty had not taken her out often of late. Her flight feathers had grown brittle and her molts had become less frequent, the regrowth thinner each time. And just as an old person often shrinks in stature, Moss's talons had shortened so much they looked more like chicken claws than the talons of a bird that was once the scourge of large hares. But while the faculties upon which a bird is so dependent seemed to have weakened, other aspects of Moss's being seemed to have grown stronger. She had become even more sensitive, almost intuitive. She could anticipate what Matty was about to do, as well as the other birds' behaviors. With stalwart Ulysses, Moss and her powers of intuition, and Marigold, so bold and aggressive, Matty felt that she could not be in better company or with stronger allies.

Moss now perched on her left shoulder, Marigold on her right, and Ulysses in his watch position high over the roof of the tree house. Matty looked up through the canopy at the immense goshawk. His broad shoulders were squared and he had a keen look in his red eyes. She turned to Moss and spoke softly in the strange language that she shared with her hawks. "Four birds we are," Matty whispered, "all perched in a tree. Moss and Marigold on my shoulders and me on a limb and Ulysses on the roof of my lovely little house."

She no longer attached their jesses when they went out. It was her own version of the golden rule. They would never tether her, and she would never tether them.

It began to rain softly, and the tree house seemed cozier than ever. Once again she began to experience the sensation she had after Marigold's first flight. It began with the stirring in her shoulders. Except now that stirring did not seem so odd. She blinked and looked down at a leaf. What she thought was a small green bump or blister began to quake and a tiny worm no bigger than a pinhead squirmed out. *I am seeing like a bird.* She felt Moss turn to her, and with her beak gently begin to stroke her bare skin. *She's preening me! Have I grown feathers?*

Her skin still looked like skin and yet it felt very different. Odd? But not odd! That was perhaps the most astounding part. None of this felt peculiar or strange but so natural, as if two elements of Matty's being, of her spirit, were magically being woven together into a new living thing. But the sensation was fleeting. She felt a soft jolt and the mysterious fabric was softly torn asunder as Marigold suddenly puffed up and shivered.

Matty knew immediately that Marigold's reaction was not to the chill breeze that accompanied the rain. She could almost sense the danger herself, but not quite as her hawks were sensing it. From the top of the tree there was a *kak-kak* sound of alarm from Ulysses. Moss roused herself. Marigold seemed ready to fly off, but Moss shot her a severe glance.

Soft gurgling vocalizations drifted down from Ulysses. *"Gyruch garrrgh tosch, stasik malpee."* (Permission to fly a short reconnaisance, requested.)

"Gyruch hyeh hyeh," Matty whispered back. To any human passing it would sound no different from the clucking of a very small flock of birds.

Ulysses had barely lifted off when, from behind the scrim of the willow's branches and the soft drizzle misting over the creek, Matty saw a shadowy figure. *The shadow man? After all this time?*

"*Ptschaw, chu chu,*" she whispered, stroking Marigold's back feathers. She felt her own heart thumping loudly. A figure swathed in a dark hooded robe was approaching the creek's edge. Matty watched as the figure knelt. So intent was the person on his business that he did not notice the goshawk hovering overhead. Was it in the kneeling that something familiar struck Matty? Was it the way in which the figure nearly prostrated itself on the bank of the creek that reminded her of—something—a gesture, a peculiar posture that did not belong in this wooded land? The figure held something in its hand. Just as it reached to stuff whatever it was under the embankment the hood slipped back and the head turned quickly.

Matty's heart almost stopped. Once again she felt that terrible sensation of peering into a void. The transparent eyes bore right through the screen of willows. Matty's breath locked in her throat. This was no shadow man. This was the abbess. These were the eyes of the abbess. But, even odder, Matty knew as surely as she had ever known anything that these were the eyes that had bored into her when she had taken Marigold on her first free flight. She remembered Fynn saying that he thought the abbess might be connected to the Bishop of Hereford, and then Matty remembered Rich's words: "That makes sense. I heard, too, that there was a new abbess in the Nottingham abbey. How convenient for her to work with the sheriff. And the sheriff is owned by Prince John, who wants to own the church. Oh yes, it all begins to fit neatly, doesn't it. A devilish design of scoundrels and tyrants and rotten men of the cloth!"

But would she come all the way from Nottingham unless she had something very important to hide? Something very precious? Of course not! It made, as Rich had said, perfect sense.

Matty was not sure how long the abbess stared at the tree, but gradually she came to realize that the woman had not seen her. The abbess had been forced to twist her head and body in order to reach under the embankment. But the awful feeling, the same one she had experienced in church, washed over her again as she caught sight of those odd eyes. Nothing living had such eyes. Nothing!

Chapter 13

DOWN THE GARDEROBE AND INTO THE NIGHT

Bad temper in all living creatures can be the result of fretfulness as well as timidity or lack of confidence. This is particularly true with hawks. It therefore stands to reason that those hawks that are the best tempered are in general the boldest, the strongest, and the best fliers.

MATTY HAD BEEN so frightened that she had waited several hours until dark so she could leave her perch under the cover of the night. Her mind swirled with confusion. She must find the boys and tell them that the shadow man was no man at all but a shadow woman—the abbess. But she must first get home because her father and Meg would worry about her being out this late.

"Night hawking?" Lord William inquired as she appeared in the keep.

"Oh, just a bit. First the boys and I were out gathering flowers for the church," she lied. "You know, May nineteenth, St. Dunstan's Day, is in just two more days."

St. Dunstan had been the archbishop of Canterbury and a beloved man. In the wooded swampland the rare flowers called St. Dunstan were named for him because he had loved music and its petals were shaped like harps.

She ate some cold porridge and immediately went to her bed. Now she had to wait until everyone was asleep, which would not be long, and then she would sneak out. Matty had a tried and true, albeit smelly, method for accomplishing this. The garderobe. The garderobes, or toilets, in many castles were stacked in the outer parts of the towers. There might be one garderobe for each floor where a space had been carved out of the wall for a shaft that opened onto a pit. The pit had an access port at the base for cleaning. Rocks had been set in a steplike pattern, projected within the shaft, offering perfect hand- and footholds. It was not a pleasant journey down the fifty-foot shaft, but no one would have dreamed that a sensitive young maiden would ever subject herself to the odors and indignities of such a place in order to sneak out. But that was exactly what Matty had done on several occasions. Since she, her father, Meg, and Hodge had begun living the up-and-down life in the tower there was only one main staircase by which she could descend and on that she would be at risk of disturbing everyone.

Matty waited until she was sure everyone was soundly asleep. Even the birds were still for the night. As she reached for her cloak, Marigold stirred. But Moss, who perched next to the little merlin, moved closer and made a throaty clucking in the back of her throat as if to say *calm down, calm down. Give your mistress a moment.*

The weather had been warm, and the garderobe was very smelly. Although it was nearly dark, Matty's eyes soon accustomed themselves, and she could pick out the shapes of the stones. She had practically memorized the best handholds, and she quickly covered the first twenty feet downward. She was just beneath the second floor when she heard a shuffling sound. She froze, plastered to the reeking walls. A bit of light fell from above, then a muttering.

"Deus vult!" *God wills!* Matty mouthed the words. As old Meg sat down on the commode, Matty squeezed her eyes shut. The last thing she wanted to see was a withered bottom. Matty felt herself blushing. Had poor Meg known that Matty was frozen to the curved wall just beneath her, the old woman probably would have died of shame.

It took Meg forever to do her business and shuffle out of the garderobe. But finally she was gone. Matty lost no time getting the rest of the way down and out of the castle into the clear fresh air. She breathed a few deep lungfuls and set off in the direction of the Woodfynns' cottage.

Crouching behind the fence of the chicken yard Matty whistled softly—once, twice. After a pause, she whistled twice more. The sound, similar to the peep of a wood thrush, was the signal that she and all the boys used when they wanted to rouse one another. But there was no answer. She turned suddenly when she heard a rustling in the bushes behind her, then caught her breath as a bent figure stepped out of the brush.

"Disturbing the peace are ye!" the voice cawed.

"Oh no, madam," Matty replied. The woman carried a crook like that of a shepherd and on one arm was a basket. She was wrapped in a shawl that covered her head and was so bent over that her nose nearly touched the ground.

"How do you know I'm a madam and not a miss? And what's a decent girl like you doing abroad at night? Gets my pins in a twist to see a decent girl out at an indecent hour."

Matty was suddenly suspicious. "I might ask the same of you."

The woman suddenly dropped her crook and reared up to twice her height while sweeping off her shawl.

"Ta-da!"

"Fynn! You scoundrel!"

"Good disguise, isn't it? Got me into the royal dairy and look what I picked up—nice round of cheese. But what may I ask are you doing here, Matty? Decent lass as I was saying. Although you don't smell that lovely."

"Had to come by way of the garderobe." She paused. "Fynn," she said softly, "I have some news." She paused dramatically. "The shadow man—remember him?"

"Yes?" His eyes widened with expectation. The blueness of Fynn's eyes was remarkable even on a night dark as this.

"'Tis not a man at all but a woman."

"What?"

"'Tis the abbess we saw at church some Sundays ago."

Fynn's mouth dropped, but no words came.

Chapter 14

A STRANGER ON THE ROAD

*Long slender toes, well separated at the base, are indeed
a virtue for hawks. The wider the area a hawk's feet can
cover, the better it can seize its quarry; it is important to
take great care of a hawk's feet, for these are its weapons.
Padded perches are recommended and if in fact corns or
feet swelling develop, a fortifying lotion of eggs whites
mixed with vinegar and rosewater is suggested.*

I T WAS AGREED THAT Fynn would rouse the other
boys and the five of them would meet at a cave
near the edge of the greenwood not far from
where Matty had observed the abbess. Matty would
head straightaway to the cave. The others would fan
out, taking different routes. It was too risky for a
group to travel together. The sheriff's men had been

thick at night to catch poachers in the forests.

Soon Matty was walking down the road that bordered the field she would cut across to the greenwood. The moon, more than a sliver, less than a wedge, ducked in and out of the thick clouds that raced across the sky. Eerie tinkling sounds drifted down the road. "A leper's bell! God's knees!" Matty muttered. She had not a penny on her. Indeed, all that she had was a stale bun that she had swiped from the larder earlier that evening in case she got hungry, or rather, hungrier. She was always hungry. Meg had traded one of the two rabbits Morgana had caught the previous week for some flour and had done a bit of baking. Matty had been planning on the bun as a snack for herself. The hunched figure approached.

"Alms? Alms?" The words came out from a dark void encircled by a deep hood. A staff with a bucket attached was clutched with the remaining finger stubs on the stump of the leper's hand. The figure stopped downwind of Matty as was the rule for lepers. "Alms, milady?" The leper extended the staff with the bucket on the end.

"No alms, sir." As Matty spoke, she drew out the bun and dropped it in the bucket. She could not resist peering into the hood.

The wreckage of what was once a face hid within the shadows. The nose was gone and what remained was a single cavity through which a hissing wind blew. One eye had vanished behind a boulder of bubbling flesh.

"I am no sir, kind lady. I was a woman, once a girl like you." The woman must have had this disease for a while. Perhaps the cruelest part of leprosy was that it moved slowly, taking its victims bit by bit. Matty wondered if the woman was on her way to see Nelly Woodfynn.

"I am sorry, so sorry," Matty whispered.

"No need to be sorry, child. I am nothing now, not woman nor man, not young nor old, not human nor beast."

Pain gripped Matty's heart. For one instant she felt every shred of suffering this woman had ever experienced. "And what be your name, madam?"

The leper didn't reply immediately. Matty heard instead a sharp intake of breath, like wind whistling down a deep gorge.

"My name was Helena, kind child."

"Helena," Mattie said softly. Helena was one of

Matty's favorite saints. Daring and adventurous, she set off for the Holy Land to find the true cross. "Madam, your name is still Helena."

"God bless you, child!" But the words, like dry leaves, seemed lost on a freshening breeze.

Matty rushed off.

The boys were waiting for her at the cave. Clouds had thickened and obscured the moon, but their eyes grew quickly accustomed to the darkness and Matty, who knew the way well, led them to the creek bank near the willow tree house.

"You say, Matty, that she did not carry a shovel or spade. That she just put a parcel under the bank?" Rich asked.

"Yes, it was along here." The five of them were beneath the embankment and walking along the edge of the creek.

"It's like hunting for a needle in a haystack," Will said.

"Look, look," Fynn said suddenly. "The grass has been smashed on top and there is loose dirt all along here. Bless this abbess, she's as easy to track as a horse-drawn cart through mud. This is no shadow! I'll wager whatever she hid is right there!" He pointed to a spot where the creek had cut away deeply at the bank and the ground overhung like a shelf. He poked with a branch. "It goes back far."

"Far as an arm can reach," Matty said quietly.

"Don't seem to be any animals there. Though it might be an otter's den. Who wants to reach in?"

"I do! I do! Me!" There was a chorus of voices.

"Back off, lads!" Fynn spoke sharply. "I should never have asked. It's plain who should reach in."

There was a sudden silence. The three other boys stepped back, and then they all looked at Matty.

Matty shrugged slightly as if to say, *So now I get my due for building that tree house*. "All right," she replied, and dropped to her knees. "I wish we'd brought a torch."

"You want the whole world to know!" Hubie whispered.

Matty reached in with her arm, feeling among the twigs and debris that must have been washed in when the creek was high.

"Anything?" Will said eagerly.

"Nothing unusual." But just as she said the words her fingers touched something that was not mud or rock or wood or damp leaves. It was hard and metallic. As she ran her fingers over the top, she felt a design.

When she drew the narrow box out, they stared down at it. The lid was embossed with a design of a palm that they recognized as the symbol of pilgrims who had journeyed to Jerusalem.

"It's a reliquary box," Rich said. His voice could not belie his disappointment. They were all disappointed. The box was so small—what possible treasure could it hold save a few strands of hair or perhaps some fingernail scraps from a saint who died in the Holy Land?

"Well, open it," Will said.

Matty wiggled the lid a bit and it started to lift off. In the same moment the sky cleared and the moon, though still only a wedge, poured a stream of silver that illuminated the creek bank. They all gasped.

In the box five immense rubies glittered.

Chapter 15

BLOOD AND RUBIES

*Any falconer's medicine box should have the following
herbs and tinctures, for they will be indispensable in
treating the common maladies and maintaining your
hawks in good health: borage, germander, horse-mintes,
sage aloes, cicotrine, nightshade, and henbane.*

HE BOYS AND MATTY slipped quietly up the bank
of the creek and made their way wordlessly
through the forest until they reached the cave.

"They are the very same rubies as those on the
chalice. I swear!" Rich gasped.

"So what might that mean?" Fynn asked. "If, Rich,
as you said, the chalice was been taken for repair,
did it look the same when we last saw it in church or
different?"

"Well, if the rubies were missing, we would have noticed," Matty said.

"Certainly," Will agreed.

"Yes, I suppose so," Fynn said, rubbing his chin.

"Suppose so? I know so," Rich said firmly.

"But would you have noticed if they weren't the same rubies?" Fynn asked.

"Weren't the same rubies?" they all said at once.

"Yes, what if the silversmith substituted fake ones?"

"How do you fake a ruby, Fynn?" Hubie asked.

"I have no idea. But it seems to me if they can make stained-glass windows with ruby-colored panes—I've heard about the ones at Canterbury . . ."

"If . . ." Matty said slowly, "they can make stained-glass windows that look as red as rubies, then what Fynn is saying is that they can make fake gems out of glass that look like real ones."

"It's hard to believe that the church would do that," Will said.

"Remember the rumors about the Bishop of Hereford," Hubie said.

"Yes, the Bishop of Hereford and Prince John

together would do that," Fynn agreed. "And now think of how the abbess fits into all this."

"These rubies alone could buy the prince land and any soldiers he wanted most likely. It could be civil war and with Richard so far . . ." Matty's voice melted away.

"They could be all that stand between John and the crown," Rich said.

"A king's ransom," Matty said quietly.

"What should we do with them?" Rich asked.

"Well, we can't exactly return them to the church, can we now?" Will said.

"But we can't keep them for ourselves," Hubie replied.

Fynn looked about and then motioned them to come closer. He dropped his voice to a whisper. "These rubies cannot fall into John's hands. They will help put a villain on the throne of England. He will use them to buy an army to achieve his goal. Anything we can do to stop that is good."

"Maybe the rubies could help more people," Hubie said.

Listening to both Fynn and Hubie, an idea began

to form in Matty's mind.

"Maybe the rubies could help overthrow tyrants," Matty said. A quiet descended on the five friends. They each thought about the suffering they had seen in the past years. A stolen round of cheese or haunch of venison could go only so far. But might there be enough wealth in these rubies to stop the tyranny?

Finally Fynn broke the silence. "I see what Matty is saying. But we must bide our time. Rubies like these are not easy to trade for money. Safer to steal gold and silver from the prince or the sheriff's coffers to help the people. I think for now we should hide them, hide them well, and not all in one place, but five different places that we all know about."

Matty knew that Fynn was right about this. For now they must hide the jewels—hide them where they could never be found. Matty suddenly remembered such a place.

"There is a sickness that sparrow hawks get. It is carried by wood ticks and once a hawk gets that disease it abandons its nest."

"I know about that illness. It's as if the whole tree gets sick. The leaves turn gray and scaly," Rich said.

"The hawk leaves the tree and no other birds will nest there. And even people don't go near those trees. It's like they're haunted. The ghosts of trees long dead."

"Exactly my point," Matty said. The boys' eyes widened as they realized what Matty was really saying. "I know of five such trees in this forest. They all have hollows perfect for hiding. They are unbothered by the birds and people, and their timber is not good for firewood. They are—" She hesitated as she remembered the woman Helena she had met on the road. "They are not merely haunted or ghosts. They are the lepers of the forest. That is where we should hide the rubies." Then Matty stood back and looked grimly at each boy. "Until now I have never joined your thievery."

"Aah, don't worry about it, Matty," Rich said.

"I never worried about it, Rich, but all that was petty thievery compared to this."

"Yeah," said Fynn. "That was pickpocket, cutpurse. Now we're committing a far greater crime." He seemed to smile as he said the words.

"Well, that's the point," Matty replied. "You can count me in. I'm a robber now as well."

"Not you, Matty," Fynn said. "This is not girls' work."

Fury flared within her. "It's outlaws' work is what it is. Thieves' work. A thief can be a man, a woman, a girl, or a boy. I found the rubies!" The color had risen in her cheeks. She was not so much angry as determined for them to see her as who she was and who she knew she could be: an outlaw like the rest of them.

"I want you to trust me. We all need to trust one another. It has nothing to do with being a girl or a boy. What we've taken is not a prize hen's eggs, a round of cheese, or a deer from the royal forest. I think we need to make a blood oath, for indeed we are in possession now of unbelievable riches. So we must swear an oath of loyalty."

The four others nodded in solemn agreement. Fynn drew out his hunting knife. Each one took it, and in the dim light of the cave slashed the tips of their thumbs. They then went around and pressed their thumbs to one another's and repeated the words after Matty.

"I solemnly do swear upon this oath of blood never to reveal my knowledge of the rubies to any human being. The riches we have found will be used only in service to our lawful king, Richard, and to defeat the tyranny that prevails in this land but never for our personal gain. This I swear in the name of our Lord."

BOOK TWO

WHEN FYNN BECAME ROBIN HOOD

and

WHEN MATTY BECAME MAID MARIAN

Chapter 16

A WINTER OF DESPAIR

Cramp is a crippling condition of the feet. Young birds, eyases, are especially susceptible. Severe cold is thought to cause cramp. There is no cure.

ALL THROUGH THE SUMMER and the fall of 1191 and well into the next winter, the rubies nestled hidden in the five hollows of the trees that Matty called the lepers of the forest. The people grew poorer. Prince John grew bolder, and the five friends grew bolder as well and more desperate. Matty had proved herself an excellent cutpurse, but the takings were slimmer even from the sheriff's men.

Beyond stealing, the boys had to find ways to earn a penny here or there to help their own families, for there were mouths to feed. Rich helped his father at the mill. It had been seized by the sheriff, who forced them to grind grain at half price for the sheriff and any of his men. Similarly Will Scarloke's father, by decree of Prince John, was made to shoe the horses of the sheriff's men free of charge. Will worked in his father's forge and had started to juggle on market days in various towns to make enough money to help buy food. Hubie spent less and less time in the forest and more time helping his mother brew and deliver ale. And Fynn's father had gone lame and could no longer work as forest warden. The family relied on the money that Nelly could get for her services as a midwife and they ate what Fynn could catch.

"We have to do something!" Fynn said, pacing the cave where they often met now.

"Is it time for the gobbets?" Will asked.

The friends had, shortly after their blood oath, decided never to mention the rubies by name. They had a score of code words for the five rubies. "Rowan berries" was one, for in winter the rowan tree bore bright red berries that were used to make dyes. Another code word was "blood," another "the gobbets"; still another was "bunions." They tried to come up with words that suggested something common and not something rare or precious.

"No, not for the gobbets, but it is time for something else." Fynn had grown, it seemed, almost a head taller in the last six months. He was nearing his sixteenth birthday. He stopped pacing and ran a hand over his cheek. "We are men now. Look, I have a beard . . . or almost."

"I almost do!" Rich said.

"Me, too," Hubie and Will both said at once.

"Oooh, me, too!" Matty said with a great sigh. She hated all this carrying on about shaving and becoming men. It seemed rather childish to her. "Just tell me, Fynn—all of you—what does a beard have to do with anything?"

"Nothing really," Fynn replied, and looked her directly in the eye. "Old lady Biggle is dying, Matty. She be dying of starvation." He paused. "You see, Matty, it is time for us to act as men." He paused again. "And women," he added, taking a step closer to Matty. The color rose in her cheeks as he studied her. He was looking very deeply into her eyes as if searching for something. The awkward silence was broken by Hubie.

"Old lady Biggle be dying of heartbreak as much

as starvation," he said. "They took her son away and threw him in the sheriff's dungeon 'cause he wouldn't cobble boots for the sheriff's guard for free. The shop is closed. They have no livelihood."

"It's like me own father and the mill," Rich said. "Me mum's starving and she be expecting a baby. Baby might die before it gets born." He paused and his eyes began to well up. "And me mum might, too."

"If it's not time for the rubies, it might be time for something almost as valuable," Matty said.

The boys turned toward her. Their brows were creased in bewilderment.

"Do you know where the sheriff keeps his coffers?" Matty asked.

"Nottingham Castle. It's well fortified," Fynn replied.

"Exactly," said Matty. "You don't have a chance of getting in there. And it's where the prince stays when he comes here."

"Do *you* think you have a chance of getting in?" Fynn asked.

"Better than you," she fired back. "I can be a maid. I can work in the scullery, the laundry, serve in the kitchen."

"She's right! Fynn!" Will leaped up. "Matty could find out all sorts of things for us . . . like—like—" Rich, Hubie, and Will all were speaking excitedly.

"Like where they keep the silver!" Hubie said. "You don't think they eat from trenchers, taking their ale in wood cups like the rest of the world, do you? She's perfect for the job! Our spy. No one will suspect Matty."

Matty's eyes were bright now. But Fynn had grown very still.

Matty walked over to him. "What's wrong, Fynn? Are you mad because I thought this up?"

"No." He scowled. "But, Matty, it's dangerous. You'll be in the thick of it. You could get caught or hurt and—"

"And there is no choice!" Matty said. "You heard what Rich said about his mum and the baby. People are dying. Dying!"

"And what about your birds, Matty? Who will take care of your hawks while you serve the sheriff?" Fynn asked.

"Ooh!" Matty said softly. She hadn't thought of that. Just before everything had seemed so possible, but now . . . ?

"I will!" Rich spoke up. "I can take care of them."

"I can help, too!" Will said.

"And me!" Hubie said.

They all now turned to Fynn. He nodded slightly and then smiled. "Count me in, Matty."

"Oh, Fynn!" she cried, flinging her arms around him. She squeezed him hard and then broke away. But she had felt his lips brush her cheek, and it had sent a wonderful jolt through her. Now he was looking down at his feet and shuffling. Had she embarrassed him by this quick embrace in front of his friends? Before, her heart had soared, but now she felt mortified. The last thing she wanted to do was embarrass Fynn. She backed away several steps and, turning to the other boys, said, "Don't worry about me. Just let me get a position in the castle. I know castles and I'll figure out this one quickly. You know it won't take me long and then I can just quit, leave. Say I have to go home to take care my aged father."

"And you won't give them your real name?" Fynn asked.

"No—no, I'll call myself . . ." She paused and thought for a few seconds. "Let's see . . . how about Marian?" She looked at the leaf that Fynn had tucked into his cap. "Marian Greenleaf!"

"All right." Fynn paused "Maid Marian." He then looked at the three others. "I think I want a new name, too!"

That is so like Fynn, Matty thought. *Probably thinks I bested him coming up with this name.* He touched the peaked green hat that he had started to wear. "If Matty is to call herself Maid Marian, I shall call myself Robert Hood." He stopped and shook his head. "Sounds rather dull, actually. How about Robin? Robin Hood? More of a ring to it, don't you think?"

Hubie stood up. At barely sixteen he had become a giant of a young man, standing well over six feet with massive shoulders and hands like hams. "I have always hated the name Hubert. So I shall call myself John."

"John!" They all gasped.

"Not like Prince John!" Matty blurted out. "How could you?"

"Me grandfather was named John. He was as right and honest a man as ever lived. One bad prince shouldn't spoil a perfectly good name." He gave them a sly look now. "But if it bothers you I'll call myself Little John and you can call me Little for short. Or Tiny or Teeny or Teensy." They were all laughing now as Little John rose on his tiptoes and began cavorting around the cave, which seemed much too small for his large figure.

"And what will you call yourselves?" Robin said, looking at Rich Much and Will Scarloke.

"I am perfectly happy with my own name. Rich as in Richard. And it is *much* an honor to bear our king's name," he said, laughing.

"And you, Will?" Marian asked.

"Scarlet—Will Scarlett or just plain Scarlett?" Rich asked.

"Scarlet—one *T* please. Never fancied that second one hanging off the end," Will replied.

Chapter 17

THE THICK OF IT

A hawk's talons may grow too long if a perch is too soft and there are not enough rubbing stones. Careful coping or clipping of the talons is then required.

MAID MARIAN—THE NEW name took some getting used to. Rather like trying to wear a new pair of shoes, a bit stiff at first. For so long she had been Matty, but now in this new life she was to be Maid Marian. She tried her best to always think of herself as such, especially since she had obtained a job in the sheriff's castle at Nottingham. Before she had left for Nottingham, a plan was worked out for sending coded messages to the boys. When hired, she would smuggle Marigold into the castle and the merlin would become her winged messenger.

Within the time Marigold had been with Marian she had proven herself to be a bird of uncanny intelligence. She had, perhaps from Moss's example, developed a patience that served her well. When Marian's father had suffered a bout of catarrh the previous winter and Meg herself was ailing, Marian had had to stay close to home to nurse them both. It had been impossible for her to go out hawking, and the food supplies had dwindled to nearly nothing. Marian had decided to try a very risky strategy for getting fresh meat. Some called it "masterless hawking" or "jessless hawking."

Marian had let the birds go jessless before, but never when hunting. To attempt this risky tactic Marian had climbed with her merlin to the highest turret of the castle. Whispering in Marigold's ear in the peculiar language that she spoke to all her birds, she had launched the merlin onto the gusting winds to hunt. This might have seemed the same as the other hunting expeditions, but it was entirely different in that there was no prey in sight. The bird herself must search out the prey. Marian was more nervous than she had ever been in all the years she had worked with hawks. She trusted the little merlin, but things could go wrong. Marigold might not find prey, or perhaps she'd wander far afield and become lost.

Marian waited anxiously at the top of the turret, squinting into the distance, turning to see if the merlin might appear from another direction. By the time Marigold flew in, carrying a plump rabbit in her talons, Marian felt such relief sweep through her, such joy, that she trembled after Marigold dropped the rabbit at her feet and she extended her arm for the merlin to perch on.

And so every few days after Marian began her job in the sheriff's castle, one of the boys went to the Fitzwalter castle to tend the hawks and look for a message brought by Marigold. There had been no messages so far.

To Lord William the boys were still just "the boys." He knew them only as Fynn, Hubie, Will, and Rich, not by their new names of Robin, Little John, and Scarlet. Rich, of course, was still Rich.

A blasted oak in Nottingham's Sherwood Forest, several miles away from Barnsdale, became the boys' new official meeting place. An immense hollow had been carved from the trunk when it had been struck by lightning, and it afforded them a shelter as big as any cave. They found the tree hollow comfortable and so began spending more time in it, for they found that they could make more money as outlaws than by staying home and working. The deer were very few in this part of the forest, and so the sheriff's officers rarely patrolled near this oak. From here the boys could keep an eye on things, particularly on who came and went in and out of the sheriff's castle. It was far from Nottingham to Barnsdale, but they had managed to steal a few horses and a cob pony right out from under the sheriff's nose, which made their travels easier.

Rich now came into the hollow tree straight from the Fitzwalter castle.

"Any news?" Robin jumped up.

"No."

"It's been over a fortnight! What's she doing there?" Robin had been burning with impatience since the day Marian left.

"You have to give it time, Robin," Little John said. "Marian will let us know when she has news."

"Little's right. Give her time, Robin," Rich said. "She might be stuck scrubbing floors in the scullery and have no idea where the sheriff keeps his coffers."

Robin's face suddenly paled. "What if she's stuck in the scullery forever and can never find out anything?

Then where will we be?"

"Well, I'd say right back where we started, and we'll have to think of a new plan for how to lighten the sheriff's purse and the prince's treasury," Scarlet said as he practiced juggling six pins.

"I can't stand it," Robin muttered.

"Look, Robin," Little John said. "I have great faith in our Marian. She will send a message when she has something to say. She will. I know it. And if anybody can find out anything about where there is money and silver plate in that pile of rocks, it's Marian. She is the one who led us to the gobbets, after all."

"I've heard a bit of other news myself," Rich said.

"What's that?" Robin asked.

"'Tis said that the Bishop of Ely is coming to Nottingham."

"William Longchamp is coming?" Robin said, suddenly excited.

"Yes, the only good man left," Rich said

"Then why would he be coming?" Little John asked.

"Well, he is the chancellor after all. But there are rumors that he is trying to make peace with John," Rich said slowly.

"Oh no!" Robin groaned.

"It might not be as bad as you think," Rich said quickly. A light sparkled in his gray-green eyes.

"I don't see how it could be any worse. The only decent man, Richard's most trusted adviser, ready to make a deal with the prince."

Rich turned his head slowly and looked at each of them. "Don't you see? It could mean that Richard is coming home. And a peace must be brokered between him and his brother." He paused. "And Marian is right there!"

Now all the boys' eyes sparkled. If it was true that Richard was returning at last, this news would be brighter than any gold or silver Marian could bring them.

Marian felt lucky that her room in the castle was high in a tower of the inner ward, for it allowed Marigold not only light but also the freedom to fly away when necessary. The first floor of the tower was used for storage. The second and third floors were for the office of the steward, a most important person of the castle. Then the top floors were divided into minuscule sleeping quarters for servants. All the floors were reached by a single staircase built into the stone wall. Marian shared her quarters with two other girls. Hannah, a great hall girl—which meant she got to serve there at feasts—and Ellie, a scullery maid like Marian.

Hannah and Ellie found the new maid sweet, although she did ask an awful lot of questions that they could not answer. Marian had to be alert. It would not be good if the two girls discovered that she could read and write. She had made up a story about coming from East Anglia near Ely, which was far away. Thankfully neither Hannah nor Ellie seemed to think much of the presence of a bird in their quarters.

Today Marian was bent over a trough, scrubbing laundry in the courtyard. This was one of the lowliest jobs in the castle. She looked up as Hannah came rushing over.

"Marian, guess what? William Longchamp, the Bishop of Ely himself, is coming! You know they say he be one of the most powerful men in England."

Marian instantly stopped scrubbing. Trying to conceal her surprise she slid the palm of her wet hand over her face as if wiping away perspiration. Why would William Longchamp be visiting the sheriff? Had he, too, like the Bishop of Hereford, thrown in his lot with that miserable pawn of Prince John?

"Did you hear me, Marian?" Hannah took a step closer. "Feeling all right, dear? You look a tad peeky. I said, the Bishop of Ely is coming here."

Now Ellie came into the yard.

"Yes, I just heard the news myself. It's to be a big feast." Ellie set down another basket of laundry. "And you better do these table linens now so they'll dry in time. Have you ever seen him, Marian?"

"Who?" asked Marian blankly.

"The Bishop of Ely," Ellie said impatiently. "You must have seen him, being from Ely."

"Oh!" Marian replied quickly. "We lived outside Ely."

"You went to church, didn't you?" Hannah said.

"Oh, yes, but not often to the cathedral, just to the little parish church, you know."

"Well, we'll all be helping out. We need extra hands at the feast to be given in his honor," Hannah said.

In his honor, Marian thought. She smelled a rat. Why would the sheriff, one of the most corrupt men in England, honor one of the most *righteous* men in England, the most faithful servant of King Richard and King Richard's mother, Eleanor of Aquitaine, with a feast?

"And the prince is to be here and all," Ellie added.

Two rats! Marian thought, as Hannah chattered on. "It's to be a big feast in the great hall—mummers, and the prince is bringing three jesters."

Marian's head was spinning. This, of course, was all she had hoped for—to serve at a grand feast. One did not find out where silver plate was kept by scrubbing bedsheets and the sheriff's shirts or spending endless hours in the scullery doing all the messy kitchen work, from cutting worms out of potatoes to mopping up the blood from freshly butchered cattle. But there was more at stake here than just silver. Finally, she might have something to write the boys about! She was about to step onto the chessboard—bishop against bishop, prince against a checkmated king. Her mind had been swirling so fast that she nearly didn't catch what Hannah said next. "What's that?"

"I said that the abbess wants to meet all of us who be serving at the feast."

"Abbess? What abbess?" Marian felt her heart skip a beat. The chessboard had suddenly turned deadly.

"The sheriff's sister, the abbess of the abbey in Nottingham."

Marian tried to speak, but no words came out.

"Marian, you look like you've seen a ghost."

I have seen a ghost! Marian thought. She took a deep breath and, recovering her voice, tried to look as normal as possible. "No, it's just I didn't know that the sheriff had a sister, a sister in the church. You know I'm not from around here."

Hannah and Ellie snickered. "What's so funny?" Marian asked.

"Well, some say she is not a sister of Christ either," Hannah whispered.

"More like a lady friend of Prince John," Ellie added. They giggled.

"But, Hannah, why isn't planning the feast the steward's job? He's the one in charge of the great hall and all who serve there," Marian asked. The steward was the highest ranking member of any castle's staff and was charged with supervising not only the functions of the great hall but also those of the entire estate and household. He was no mere domestic servant, but frequently a knight. Sir Montgomery, the steward at Nottingham castle, was no exception. Marian had seen him strutting about in fine robes trimmed in fur.

Ellie replied, "The abbess likes everything just so. That's why she wants more servants. All the silver and brass has to be polished. So I heard that we are all called in to meet the abbess in the steward's chambers in the east tower within the hour."

It is as Robin said, Marian thought. *I am truly in the thick of it.*

Chapter 18

A BIRTHDAY SURPRISE

Falconry is not simply for show; to have a hawk for carrying about on one's wrist is not only senseless but vain. Hawks are spirited and independent by nature. Thus a falconer will do well to remember those qualities and appeal to them during training.

MARIAN TRIED TO PREPARE herself to look into the void of those terrible eyes. But she was not prepared to walk into the steward's chamber and see the abbess flanked by Sir Guy of Gisborne, her mother's murderer.

On the other side of the abbess was a man dressed in bishop's robes. "Who's that?" Marian whispered to Ellie. Surely the Bishop of Ely wouldn't be present for the planning of the feast to honor him.

"The Bishop of Hereford—the very good friend of the sheriff."

Marian felt her stomach turn. She swallowed and shut her eyes tightly against the nausea. *Steady! Steady!* she told herself. *This is precisely why you are here.* Gold and silver were suddenly secondary to what she might see and find out.

The steward had begun to address the fifty-odd servants who stood before him in the castle library when he was interrupted by the abbess. From the grim look on his face it was fairly obvious that the abbess had encroached on his domain.

"This is to be a grand feast," she said, raising her hand and gracefully inscribing an arc in the air. Marian noticed that the abbess wore a large ring on her finger. Nothing fancy. No gemstones. But bigger than the simple gold ring that a nun received after her solemn vows signifying her marriage to Jesus Christ. "It is a feast in honor of King Richard's chancellor, the Bishop of Ely."

The abbess kept talking. Marian tried to listen closely but she could not stand to look at her or Sir Guy.

And now the abbess was talking about the gold

platters on which the roasted swans would be served, as well as the ducks and the suckling pigs. In addition a boar and an ox were to be roasted, sliced, and served with apples. There were silver platters on which the sugar sculptures would be served, then cheeses and nuts. The best of wine was to be poured in the French gold goblets.

Marian suddenly remembered that her father had had a secret compartment in his chamber where he kept a few silver pieces and jewels. She thought of her mother's Star of Jerusalem and felt a stitch in her heart when she remembered the flare of the white rays against the blue. If only the Star of Jerusalem had been tucked away and not on a chain around her mother's neck. (Much of the Fitzwalter treasure had been hidden behind ledgers containing the castle records. If one pushed a scroll entitled *Oat Yield, 1140–1170,* the entire shelf mysteriously swung open. Perhaps this room, too, had a secret place.)

Marian began to examine the room as closely as she could from where she was standing. She scanned the innumerable shelves of books looking for titles that might not seem just right, books that might be out of place—and perhaps not be books at all, but a disguise for a secret compartment. She read the names on the book spines. *Northumbria Tax Ledgers*, *Vassals of East Anglia*, *Collections of the Exchequer of Westminster*. The titles held little meaning beyond showing that they were helpful tools for robbing the people. But then one title caught her eye. *St. Basil's Book of Prayer*. *Prayers and taxes! Not like bread and butter*, Marian thought.

"Come on, Marian." She felt Hannah pull her arm. "You're in some dreamworld. We are to step forward and receive the bishop's blessing."

One by one the servants were quickly kneeling and kissing the bishop's hand as he made the sign of the cross over their heads.

As Marian waited, a plump man dressed in the rough brown fabric came up to her side.

"Are you a bibliophile, mademoiselle?" He spoke with a slight French accent.

"A w-what?" Marian stammered.

"I noticed you perusing the sheriff's library."

Marian had a sudden sinking feeling. Why had she not been more careful? She looked at him shyly and, affecting her best rustic accent, said, "Oh sir, I never seen books before. I don't know me letters. Can't read but barely my name."

"Really, my dear?" He bent forward slightly, and Marian took a step backward.

"Yes, sir, really. I be a scullery maid." He looked down at her hands that, although rough, did not look anything close to the ruddy, coarse, and calloused hands of Ellie, who had spent most of her life scrubbing in noblemen's castles.

Please, dear Lord, do not let me be found out. Please Lord.

"And what is your name child?"

"Marian, sir."

"Well, I am Frere Tuck, or Friar Tuck, as you say in English. I'm an old acquaintance of Prince John's mother."

"Queen Eleanor?"

"Yes, my dear. But now I serve here in the chapel of Nottingham castle."

"Oh" was all that Marian could think to say.

"Ah!" He nodded toward the Bishop of Hereford. It was her turn to kneel. Marian sank to her knees and was about to kiss the bishop's hand when her eyes opened in horror. Yes, there was a ring—a bishop's ring with its purple amethyst set in gold, symbolic of the bishop's vows of fidelity to the church, but on the little finger of the same hand there was a blazing jewel that put the dusty violet of the bishop's stone to shame. In the very center of the ring was the Star of Jerusalem.

Marian closed her eyes and saw the blood dropping from the chain in the hand of Gisborne. Everything from that horrible day rushed back. The drops of blood from her mother's throat, the pounding of the stones against the old mews tower, the frantic screeches of the birds, her father's anguished sob: "My wife murdered, and now my hawks. What next? My king? Where is my king?" Marian felt her cheek hit the floor. But her last thought before she lost consciousness was *Today is my birthday, my fourteenth birthday!*

"She's fainted. . . . She's fainted." The sound seemed to come from somewhere far away.

Someone was patting her face with a wet cloth. She did not want to open her eyes. "She'll be fine . . . fine." It was the soft, accented voice of the friar. She looked up. His large face was leaning over hers.

"I thought she looked kind of peaky out in the courtyard," Hannah was saying.

"I'm—I'm fine. Don't worry," Marian said.

"Now what's your name, child?" the friar asked.

"Mat—Marian. Marian Greenleaf."

"Well, Marian Greenleaf, I think a sip of this might prove restorative."

He took a flask out from a pouch in the folds of his robe, uncorked it, and put it to her lips. She took a tiny sip. It burned her throat, but it did revive her. "She'll be right as rain," the friar said.

"Oh, yes, I do want to serve at the feast," Marian replied.

"Of course you do, my dear. Such a festive occasion it will be. The Bishop of Ely coming . . ." Then, under his breath, "Can King Richard be far behind?"

Chapter 19

A MESSAGE DELIVERED

*A decoction of boiled rhubarb is an excellent cure for a
cold. Yes, hawks like humans do get colds.*

"ALL RIGHT, LITTLE. WHAT does the code say for
the word *sparrow*? What would that be?" Robin
was bent over the small piece of parchment that
Marigold had flown back to the mews with. He had
nearly exploded with excitement when Scarlet came
into the tree hollow shouting, "A message! A message
from our Maid Marian!"

"How do you spell it now?" Little asked.

"S-P-A-R-R-O-W," Robin said.

Little took the code key. "It's more than just one

word. Let's see." Little wrinkled his brow and scratched letters with a twig in the dirt. "Oh, by the saints!" He exhaled softly.

"What is it?"

"The abbess. Double *r* translates to double *b*—she's there at the castle. Wait, let me see the rest of that." Little leaped up and snatched the parchment from Robin. Looking between it and the code key, he began scratching madly in the dirt. The other three boys hovered over his broad shoulders. "It says that the abbess is at the castle. She be the sister of the sheriff!"

"I knew she was no-good scum from the first time I ever laid eyes on her," Scarlet blurted.

Little continued. "Marian says that the Bishop of Ely is coming and most likely Prince John."

"That we knew already," said Scarlet.

"Listen to this. They're putting on a great feast. Mummers and all."

"Mummers!" Scarlet said excitedly.

"That's what she says."

"She says she thinks she knows where to find the secret cabinet, but she's been polishing silver and gold goblets for more than a day." Robin's eyes opened wide as Little John translated the code more rapidly now. "She says that she is sure that Richard is on his way home."

Now the boys' faces turned radiant.

"Then it's true." Little John looked up. "What we suspected is true."

The boys all broke into a huge cheer. Slapping one another's shoulders they hooted and hollered.

"I knew she'd come through. I knew our Marian would come through!" Robin said, his eyes dancing like two blue stars in the dimness. "Now I have an idea." His face became very serious.

"What's that?" Scarlet asked.

"You're part of it, Scarlet. We have to get someone into the castle to help Marian. Scarlet, you're the perfect person. You're a juggler."

"Aaah!" the two other boys said at once.

"Brilliant! Robin, just brilliant!" Rich said with a hush of admiration.

"But what do you say, Scarlet? Can you get into the castle?"

"Of course. I just have to find out which troupe of mummers is going. Most likely the Plowboys from east of Nottingham; I've played with them before. Shouldn't be a problem. They always need a good juggler. And, of course, the ladies do love me." Scarlet grinned.

"I'm sure you'll quickly become a favorite of the abbess!" Robin replied.

Chapter 20

THE POISON RING

If a wild hawk is acquired at a very young age and never hunted, it must be taught to kill.

THE GREAT HALL WAS decked with banners, and hundreds of candles gleamed along the walls. There were heralds in velvet and gold cloth who marched into the hall with their horns to announce the honored guests. The guests were followed by their pages and squires, all turned out in their finest livery. It was a glittering array of plumed hats, gold and silver cloth, and velvet robes trimmed in fur. The women wore gowns with jewel-encrusted bodices. These were the lords and ladies who had survived by swearing allegiance to Prince John. Marian had never seen anything like it. And, in a country so poor that most people were starving, Marian marveled at a table laden with so much. Even in better times at the Fitzwalters' castle for St. Stephen's feast—the beginning of the celebration of the twelve days of Christmas—there had not been this much. There were two large boars and at least a half dozen suckling pigs. There were roasted swans with their feathers reattached, haunches of venison, and chicken with marybones, the marrow bones of veal and lamb. How Marian longed for a marybone. They were so rich that they were a meal in themselves.

One course after another was on the table, a dozen or more in all. Marian stood behind one of the footmen, who himself stood behind the guests on the east side of the long table. Her job was to fetch whatever he told her to bring. The footmen poured the wine and made sure every plate was kept full.

There were forty or more people at the table, including Prince John and the men and women of his court, including Sir Guy of Gisborne. Marian, of course, was not attending them in any way, but her footman, Edgar, served the Bishop of Ely. Edgar was not the brightest of footmen. Marian was surprised that the abbess had appointed him to attend this distinguished guest who, next to the prince, was the

most significant person at the feast. The Bishop of Ely
sat between Friar Tuck and the abbess. The Bishop of
Hereford sat nearby, next to the sheriff and his wife.
Every time the Hereford bishop lifted his wine goblet,
Marian could see the blaze of the Star of Jerusalem. It
incensed her. But she could not let her anger distract
her. She must pay attention to Edgar, who was rather
sloppy in his service and less than attentive. Marian
had to remind him several times to refill the Bishop of
Ely's goblet as well as Friar Tuck's.

The understeward gave the signal indicating that it
was time for the dessert. It was a chestain, or chestnut
pudding, sprinkled with blawn powder. Just carrying
it in whetted Marian's appetite, for the scents of
cinnamon, nutmeg, and sugar were irresistible. It had
been so long since she had tasted such treats.

The mummers would perform soon. The footmen
had been instructed to extinguish most of the torches
and candles, for the mummers themselves would be
juggling with fire and spinning flame wheels as part of
the performance. As Edgar stepped away to perform
this task, Marian had a clear view of the abbess. The
ring she wore was quite large. It appeared to Marian to
resemble the type of crusader ring known as the Cross

of the Holy Land, which was a locket mounted on a band and designed to carry a relic.

The great hall darkened. The shadowy figures of the mummers could be spotted taking their places. In the dark sliver of time, between the torches' extinguishing and the first mummers rushing in with their lighted juggling, Marian saw the abbess flick open the ring on her finger. Everyone else's attention was now riveted on the jugglers' fire clubs that were whizzing through the air like comets. But Marian froze as she saw the abbess take a pinch of a powdery substance from the ring and sprinkle it on top of the Bishop of Ely's trifle. Amid the flashes of the fiery clubs, the oohs and aaahs of the audience, Marian realized what had just occurred. *The abbess is poisoning the Bishop of Ely.*

Marian realized that if the bishop ate it he would be doomed, yet she felt paralyzed. What was she to do? Edgar had not yet returned to his post and she had been left to hold the silver wine decanter. Soon the bishop would take his first bite. She stepped forward tentatively. What could she do? Her mind was blank. Then she felt herself trip. "Oh, Deus Vult!" she swore. She was crashing into the table. The pitcher slipped from her hands. There were yelps from the abbess, who jumped up, as well as from the bishop and Friar Tuck.

"Oh, forgive me! I don't know what happened, your grace." And that was the truth. Marian didn't know what had happened.

"No harm done! No harm done!" Friar Tuck said, quickly using his sleeve to help to mop the bishop's robe. The accident had not seemed to disturb the audience, who were entranced by the mummers' increasingly daring stunts.

"Who are you, you clumsy girl?" The abbess was in a rage.

"It's nothing, good lady, nothing. Don't fault the child. She meant well, I am sure. No harm," Friar Tuck said immediately.

Precisely. No harm, Marian thought as she looked down at the bishop's plate.

"No harm," repeated Friar Tuck. "Now why not clear that plate away, my dear. Throw out the trifle— no one wants wine-soaked trifle—can't taste the blawn powder—the best part." He chuckled and patted his own ample belly. "Bring the bishop a fresh one."

"Oh, no need. I have had quite enough," the bishop said, turning to the abbess. "Superb feast, Abbess. Superb."

But Marian was not looking at the abbess, who had for all appearances turned to stone. She was looking at Friar Tuck. She knew exactly what had happened: Friar Tuck had tripped her. His right foot was splashed with wine.

"I suggest," the abbess said coldly, "that this serving girl be retired for the rest of the evening. I cannot tolerate an ox as a maidservant. The only oxen in the great hall are roasted and served with apples." She narrowed her eyes and talked directly at Marian.

Marian felt herself grow faint. She wavered a bit. *I have to get out of here.* She was still clutching the silver pitcher as she ran from the great hall into the lesser hall of the castle where the mummers were practicing their next tricks.

Chapter 21

FIRE OR DUNG?

When a hawk's mutes, or droppings, change from white to green and the hawk seems listless, it is a sign of a digestive ailment. Such ailments are best cured by feeding the bird freshly killed game with its feathers or fur attached to provide roughage.

As MARIAN ROUNDED THE corner, she slammed into a tall figure in a red cloak. "Scarlet!" she gasped. Scarlet clapped a hand over her mouth and dragged her off to a shadowy corner.

"You're here!" she exclaimed when he removed his hand.

"Yes, Marian, and so are you. Fancy us meeting like this! Don't have much time. About to go on with the second round of jugglers. What is it?"

"I'm in trouble!"

"Well, I probably will be soon. What's that you got?" Scarlet looked down at the pitcher she was clutching to her chest.

"Oh, good heavens, I forgot to take it back to the kitchen."

"Why take it back? Bet it could fetch a fine price."

Marian blinked. He was right, of course. "Take it!" She tried to shove it into his hands.

"No, you take it. I have to perform. But where else is there treasure?"

"Look, hardly time for treasure. The abbess just tried to poison the Bishop of Ely and I . . . well I . . . managed to stop it. She's furious. I've got to get out of here."

Marian looked over her shoulder. She caught sight of the abbess storming into the hall. "She's after me! I have to go." She ducked behind Scarlet, and as she ran she heard an angry voice boom.

"Has anyone seen a serving girl carrying a silver pitcher? She is called Marian."

"Oh, yes. I saw her." Scarlet stepped forward. "I passed her as I left the great hall. She was on her way to the kitchen, she said."

* * *

Marian had just sent Marigold back to the Fitzwalter castle and packed up her own small bundle of clothes with the silver pitcher wrapped in a spare kirtle. She was leaving her quarters when she heard footsteps mounting the staircase. Now she pressed herself against the wall. *Would that I could fly, too!* she thought as the sound of footsteps grew louder. A shadow sliced across the pool of yellow light cast by the candle. *She's coming for me now!*

And then the abbess was there on the staircase just a few steps below where Marian stood.

"Oh!" the abbess said in a mocking voice. "Not simply a spy but a thief as well." She nodded at the bundle Marian held. The silver handle of the pitcher was clearly visible.

But not a murderess! Marian thought.

Marian stood frozen.

"Lost your tongue, did you?" The abbess's lips pulled back into a rictus that looked like a skull trying to smile. The abbess slowly started to advance upon her.

"You know what the sheriff does to thieves, don't you?" The abbess raised her rather thick eyebrows as if awaiting a response. Still Marian said nothing. Then brightly the abbess chirped almost with merriment. "Their hands! Yes, first offense only one hand. Usually, he just has the swordsman chop off the left if one is right-handed. He's quite merciful. Second offense, the right hand goes. Third offense . . . well, we shouldn't talk about that, but what's a thief without his—or should I say, her—eyes?" The abbess paused. "And spies . . . yes, spies would certainly be out of business with no ears."

She is dismembering me as I stand here! And with each slice of the abbess's tongue, she took a step closer to Marian. *I have to stop this!*

Without thinking, Marian slung her bundle in a wide sweeping arc and knocked the candle over. A sheet of flame leaped down the steps, igniting the rushes and dried grasses that covered the floor. There was a piercing shriek. Marian turned and ran up the spiraling staircase. There was no way down except the garderobe! *Not again!* Marian slipped into the portal of the garderobe and then began her descent. *Fire or dung? Not much of a choice,* she thought miserably.

Chapter 22

OUTLAWS

Frounce is a severe illness contracted by hawks when they eat pigeons. The first sign is a yellowish growth in the mouth. Therefore it is necessary to periodically examine your hawk's mouth.

M ARIAN'S FATHER SAT SLUMPED in a chair and stared at her as she stood before him. She had just returned from Nottingham. Her father had not said a word. *Of course he doesn't recognize me,* Marian thought. *I smell like a dung heap.* But there was a distant, foggy look in his faded eyes. His lips began to tremble and move, but no sound came out. Meg stood tensely by his side. "Who are you?" Lord William spoke in a tremulous voice.

"It's Matty, Lord William. Your daughter, Matty.

Remember," Meg said, "she's been gone for a bit. She got herself a job in Derby."

"Yes, Father, it's me, Matty." For more than a month she had been called Marian, but hearing her father's voice, she was Matty again. She went over to him and dropped to her knees. "I know I'm all dirty. But, see, I did bring back some money." She dug into her bundle, careful not to reveal the silver pitcher, and brought out two handfuls of coins. "I earned these, Father. "

"Oh, your mother won't approve of a lovely maiden touching coins. Oh dear, she'll be very upset when she comes down for supper."

Marian cast a desperate glance at Meg.

"He's been like this since day before yesterday," Meg whispered.

"Meg, where is my real daughter? This girl, I think, has come to help you in the kitchen. Is Michaelmas coming? We'll need extra help. Yes, you know how Lady Suzanne is."

Marian got up from her knees and backed away. She'd have Meg heat some water for her to wash. Perhaps tomorrow he would recognize her, she thought tiredly. But first she had to get to the mews and see if Marigold had returned.

The birds knew her despite the odors of the garderobe. They seemed happy that she was back, although she could tell that the boys had taken excellent care of them. Every perch had been scraped and sanded. There were new rushes on the floor.

When she went back downstairs, Meg had hot water ready. As Marian sat in the wood tub, washing, Meg said, "Lord William must have taken a seizure like Hodge."

"Oh, dear Meg. I am so sorry." Marian was filled with sadness and not just for her father. "It must be so lonely for you here now."

"Well, you're here now, dearie. Won't be quite so lonely. How was Derby?"

Marian looked up suddenly. "Meg, it wasn't Derby, it was Nottingham. I went and worked right in the sheriff's castle."

"You didn't!" Meg gasped. "Now you've given me such a shock, I'll take a fit like your father and old Hodge."

"I did it for all of us. I can't explain just yet. But, Meg, I am in a bit of trouble. It would be best that you not tell anyone that I was working in Nottingham castle."

"Yes, but you told us that you were going to Derby. Why, Derby's almost out of the shire."

"I lied." She looked steadily at her kind old nursemaid.

Tears sprang into Meg's eyes. "There only be one reason why a lovely girl like you comes home smelling like dung. You did it for all of us, as you said. God bless you."

"You'll keep it a secret, won't you?"

"Of course, Matty. But what was the trouble that you got into?"

"It's best you don't know. But if anybody comes here asking where I've been, just say I've been here tending my father who's been taken ill."

"Don't worry, dear. Don't worry. And if anyone asks me where I got these coins, I'll say that Robin Hood gave them to me."

Robin Hood? Marian was about to say, when at that moment they heard a pounding on the door. Marian hopped out of the tub and wrapped herself in a heavy blanket before the door flung open.

"Rob—" Marian blurted. "Fynn!"

Meg planted herself right in front of him. "Matty ain't decent, Robert Woodfynn. Ye got no business in here when she be half naked."

"It's all right, Meg. I'm more covered with this blanket than I am in my kirtle and cloak."

"So you got out all right! Scarlet said a fire broke out." He looked nervously at Meg.

"Don't worry, she knows," Marian said. "But how did Scarlet get out and back so fast?"

"He stole one of the sheriff's men's horses."

"Really!" The blanket dropped from her shoulder as she gave a start. Meg plucked it up and covered her shoulder, muttering about what Lady Suzanne would say if she saw her daughter now.

Robin grinned and took a step back, blushing slightly.

"Wait here. Let me get dressed. I'll be back quickly. I have something to show you."

"Yes, that's what Will said." He cocked his head toward Meg as if to warn Marian.

"It's all right. She won't mind."

"Won't mind what?" Meg asked. But Marian was already racing toward the spiraling stairs to the mews.

When she returned, she was holding the silver pitcher.

"By God's precious heart, what have you done, Matty?" Meg asked.

Marian set down the pitcher on the table and walked over to Meg, who could not take her eyes from the gleaming vessel. "I stole it. 'Tis true, Meg, but Rob—Fynn—will take it and sell it. And watch, the money he gets for it will come back to the people."

"She's right, Mistress Meg. And Scarlet managed to filch a goblet or two when he wasn't juggling. So there'll be more!"

"What in the name . . ." Meg put her hand to her brow as she looked at the two young people. After a moment, she threw her hands in the air and declared, "I don't want to know." Her face was proud and troubled as she left the room.

Marian clapped her hands. "It was worth it, wasn't it, Robin, me being the maid and all that."

"It certainly was, and from what I understand you managed to save a bishop's life as well."

"Yes, but there is another one I have not settled my score with yet," Marian said darkly.

"Oh?" Robin lifted an eyebrow.

"I'll explain tomorrow. Let's meet at the cave in Barnsdale."

"We're not at the cave anymore. We more or less live at the blasted oak."

"The one near Sherwood? But it's so far. Why not the cave?"

"It's better. And we've made platforms like the tree houses in Barnsdale. None as nice as the one you made in the weeping willow."

"I had to make it by myself because you kept me out, remember? But how did you come back and tend the birds?"

"Well, we already had some horses. So that made it easy. And I got a fine little cob pony you can ride. You see, while you were away—"

"But I was only away for a bit over a month."

"A lot can happen."

"So that's why you had to find a new hideout because they know about you in Barnsdale?"

"Yes, and they'll never expect us right under their noses in Nottingham. It's a good place. We're safer than the sheriff in his castle. For you see we know where he is, but he doesn't know where we are. It's like they say in chess—'A knight on the rim is dim,' since it can only attack half the squares from the edge of the chessboard than it could from the center. Better to be in the center."

But are we knights or outlaws? Marian wondered. *Or outlaw knights, perhaps?* She took a deep breath. "I guess we're . . . um . . . true outlaws now," she said softly. *"Outlaws."* The word rang in her head. Her pulse quickened. "Robin," she said softly.

"Yes?"

She decided she couldn't wait until tomorrow to tell him. "There's something I saw when I was at the castle. Something I want back."

"Want back?" he asked with a trace of confusion. "Something of yours?"

"My—score—I told you it's unsettled with the Bishop of Hereford. It's the bishop's ring."

"His ring? The bishop's ring? I don't understand."

"Not the ring of his church office. No. The stone in my mother's pendant, the Star of Jerusalem, he now wears in a ring. I plan to steal it back, Robin Hood. We're outlaws after all."

Chapter 23

TO TAKE A BISHOP

When a hawk completes its first molt, it acquires a new dignity. This perhaps has to do with the dawning realization of its own powers of flight, of its ability to hunt, overtake, and kill. No longer will it tolerate a stranger stroking its wings.

WITH THE RUMORS OF Richard's impending return, Prince John began his final and most desperate efforts to rally his forces. He needed money for bribes, food for his soldiers, weaponry, horses, and all manner of equipment with which he was determined to defeat his brother. What was not given willingly he took by force. But another force had emerged that perhaps at first did not seem so significant. It was a band of outlaws. These were outlaws like none had ever known, for they stole silver and gold from those few families who remained rich because of their allegiance to the prince and the sheriff and gave to the desperately poor. Throughout the countryside these outlaws who always robbed with good cheer were known, as Meg had mentioned the night Marian had returned from Nottingham, to be led by a certain Robin Hood. They were called Robin Hood and his Merry Men. No one suspected that one of the Merry Men—in fact, their chief strategist—was a girl.

Marian had completed her first real "molt" soon after she returned to her castle from Nottingham. She had cut her hair short and now wore leggings with a tunic that fell to mid thigh. On her head she wore a loose hood. She had sewn these garments herself of a green cloth that blended well with the forests.

Although she had planned to go to the blasted oak within days of her coming home from the sheriff's castle, her father's condition had worsened. She rarely left his bedside. She was not sure if he could hear her words, but she spoke to him as she held his hand. Sometimes he gave her fingers a slight squeeze, but those times became fewer and farther apart. Then one cold and moonless night she felt his hand clasp hers firmly.

"Look, Matty!" he whispered hoarsely, his eyes opened wide. He nodded as if to direct her attention toward something outside. There, framed in the window against the midnight blue of the sky, a star shone fiercely. The Star of Jerusalem! She fastened her eyes on the milky streaks that stretched the star's rays of light into a perfect cross. A voice in her head whispered something from the day her mother had died: *Keep looking into this deep blue . . . we shall be safe. It will be the sky, and we will be little stars and float . . . float away . . . away.*

She felt her father's grip slacken. "Father?" But she knew, though his eyes were still open, that he had gone.

She slid her fingertips over his eyelids to close them, for the star had quickly passed out of the window and taken her father with it. Her dear, dear father who had taught her the way of hawks, taught her to read and to write, to use a needle to mend a broken feather shaft. He had taught her all this in a time when no wellborn lady was supposed to know any such things. A time when to dance a fine saltarello was considered vastly more important than reading. A time when to figure mathematical calculations was a suspect skill only for shrewish women of trade. A time when needles were used only to embroider. He had been both a father and mother to her.

Marian was alone now. The hawks and Hodge and Meg depended on her. The Fitzwalter castle, long plundered, was of no further interest to the sheriff's men, so at least they would be able to live out their remaining years there.

For days Marian remained in the castle. She did not cry. She felt it important to fight any such feminine weaknesses. She took care of her hawks and hunted with them daily. It was as if she were determined to exercise more than ever the skills her father had taught her. But each night when she went to bed she looked out the window, searching the sky for the star that had appeared right before her father had died.

One evening she went to her father's library where she had first learned to read and took down a volume of astronomy. She knew very little about the stars and how they passed through the heavens and wondered if she might find the one that had made its transit on that night. She was not sure how long she had been reading when she was aware of a presence in the room. She turned around slowly on the stool where she sat.

"Robin!"

"I came as soon as I heard about your father. I was in the south and only heard when I got back."

"Oh, Robin!" And now the tears that had been locked somewhere deep inside were undammed. Her face was wet as Robin pressed her head against his chest. She loved the coarseness of the tunic against her cheek and the forest fragrance of his skin beneath it.

"Cry, my maid, cry!"

Marian was not sure how long she cried, or how long he held her in his arms, but finally she pushed back. She wiped her nose on her sleeve and snorted loudly, then chuckled softly. "Fine lady I would make."

"Lady enough," Robin replied.

"And reading, too!" she added, making a wry expression and nodding at the book.

"And what are you reading?"

"Astronomy."

"Astronomy? Why astronomy?"

"Looking for the Star of Jerusalem."

"Well, there is one no farther than the Bishop of

Hereford's finger, I believe."

"Yes indeed!" Marian replied, brightly now. "It is time I put my mind to that piece of business."

"Then come with me back to Sherwood and the blasted oak. I'll have some of the younger boys bring food for Meg and Hodge and your birds—they'll be provided for. We miss you, Marian." He paused. "I mean, I miss you!"

Marian had been back at the blasted oak for the better part of a week, but they had yet to come up with a plan that suited her for taking the Star of Jerusalem from the Bishop of Hereford's finger.

"When we do it, it must be done right!" Marian stood in the sputtering light of the small fire where they had just roasted some grouse. Marigold was perched on her shoulder, but Marian was thinking of Ulysses. She had learned many lessons from her hawks, but from Moss and Ulysses she had learned perhaps the most valuable ones for her new life as an outlaw: patience, discipline, and precision. For the boys, the robberies were adventures. They delighted in adding a flourishing touch in the form of a practical joke that deflated the self-importance of their victims. There was a pompous parish priest who had been hoarding food supplied to him by the sheriff while his parishioners were starving. One Saturday night, the boys stole as much as they could from his larder. The next morning after the robbery, when parishioners found the pulpit empty, they went to the priest's house and found him trussed like a pig with an apple stuffed in his mouth. He was not harmed in the least, simply humiliated.

As their reputation grew so did their numbers. More and more young men, some still just boys, joined their ranks. And, indeed, the friar from Nottingham castle had become one of their most trusted confidants. Friar Tuck moved seamlessly between the outlaws and the innermost circles of Nottingham castle, the court of Prince John, and the church.

Only the original band lived in the great oak in Sherwood, but they had developed a wide system of communication. Tree hollows, empty wells, an abandoned shepherd's hut became the places where messages were left—not all written. Some messages were given through the seemingly innocent arrangements of objects. A row of three stones with a molted feather stuck under the first stone meant a baron would be traveling abroad on the third day of the week on the high road out of Nottingham and an ambush was planned. Every village and town from Barnsdale to Nottingham, from Haworth to Porlock, now had its share of Merry Men who could contribute to such an ambush.

Now the five friends gathered in the spacious hollow of the blasted oak. Marian had added a homey touch, bringing with her an old carpet from her mother's chamber and even an embroidery to hang on the wall. Robin had of course objected, claiming she was turning it into a lady's chamber. "Precisely," Marian had retorted, "a lady's chamber and not a robber's den." A candle stuck in the neck of a jug cast a pool of light.

"Now what do you mean by *right*?" Little John asked.

"Maybe *right* is not the word, but stealing from a parish priest's larder is easy compared to taking a ring from a bishop's finger."

"We could just take the finger with it!" Little John said, flashing his dagger.

"Not if we can help it," Marian said. "Trussing a priest like a pig is one thing; chopping off fingers seems—seems a bit much."

"And it's not funny," Robin said. "You know we have a reputation to keep up. Merry Men, not monsters."

They all laughed at this. But while they were joking Marian had a thought. To take a bishop required cunning and subtlety. She thought of Robin's explanation when he had first told her about the blasted oak: "A knight on the rim is dim." This was indeed a chess game and now they were getting to the middle of the board. A bishop's moves compared to a knight's were very restricted. A knight was also the only piece that could jump other pieces. A rook, however, one of the most important pieces, plays a role usually when the middle game has been reached. *Now supposing,* Marian thought, *we are the knights, but when we get to the middle, the rooks come in, our rooks—my hawks!*

"Here is my idea," Marian said. "I heard in the marketplace the other day that the bishop comes every fortnight to dine with the abbess. He takes the north road. There is a huge oak at the big bend."

"I know the one," Robin said. "Go straight into the woods from that tree and you can get some of the best venison in all England. The two deer I brought down last week and gave away to those families up beyond Chillingham village came from there."

"That's the idea!" Marian said.

"What's the idea?" Robin asked.

"We go and kill a fat deer. That's our opening move. But instead of dressing it in the forest, we drag it to the side of the road and dress it by that tree."

"What, are you crazy?" Scarlet said. "He'll stop and arrest us."

"Yes. You see, we are the lure." She looked at Marigold perched on her shoulder and stroked her wings. A faraway look came into her eyes. She thought back to when she had first trained Marigold to fly to the lure by swinging those bloody lark wings. "We are first the lure and then *we* become the hawk and will fly to the fist, the fist of not a falconer but of the villain, the bishop, and I will take his ring."

Robin looked at Marian. "She knows her business. We do as Marian says. And, mind, we will get her mother's jewel."

Robin's words stirred her heart. It was a profound respect. Tears threatened her eyes. Robin was at last treating her as an equal.

Chapter 24

TO THE FIST

*When attempting to first get a hawk to fly to the fist
while tethered, do not expect the bird to stand docilely on
her perch. The bird will bate at first . . . but leave the bird
to work things out for herself.*

"No! No! THAT'S NOT how a shepherd wears his
cloak, Scarlet," Marian scolded gently. The
five of them were gathered by the oak at
the roadside. They were dressed in gray clothes of
rough-woven fabrics. She adjusted the cloak around
Scarlet's shoulders, then turned to help Robin. Her
fingers had worked nimbly with Scarlet's cloak, but
now she suddenly seemed all thumbs. She could see
some dark reddish hairs curling from the neckline of
his tunic.

"If you didn't have a mustache," he whispered, "I might kiss you!"

Her hands began to tremble. She was trying to knot the ties of his cloak but made a mess of it. Did he notice? Was she blushing? To cover her acute discomfort she spoke testily. "Don't be a fool! It's not a time for jokes."

"You mean that mustache is real?"

She gave up on attempting to fix the cloak and stood back and looked at him. Trying to sound as cold as possible but fighting a smile, she pointed at the shepherd's crook he held.

"Robin, don't carry your crook like a sword. It's for herding, not fighting—not yet at least. Now, where's the deer?"

"Off in that brush," Robin said, nodding at a thicket of brambles.

Marian looked up at the pale January sun, peering through woolly clouds. "It must be close to noon. The bishop should be here soon. So bring the deer over and we can start to dress it."

Snow flurries spun through the air, but their heads were protected by the deep hoods that not only offered a shield from the wind but also concealed their faces in shadows. Marian had used tallow to stick a few wisps of her own hair above her lip in a fair approximation of a youth's first hint of a mustache. This robbery involved a very complicated strategy, and Marian had employed nearly every lesson she had ever learned in falconry. She was setting up a lure for the bishop—the lure of a forbidden deer protected in the prince's royal forest—but at the same time she herself would have to fly to the fist. The fist with the ring that held her mother's jewel. On this mission Marigold and Ulysses were flying lookout. If things got nasty, Marian would give them the sign to attack.

"They must be coming!" Marian said as she spotted her hawks melting out of the sky.

Little John crouched and put his ear to the road. "I hear hoofbeats. There be at least a dozen men on horses."

And just five of us here! Marian thought. But there were other boys hidden throughout the growth that bordered the forest. At the first blast of Robin's horn they would come forth and fight.

"Get busy," Robin ordered. He unsheathed his blade and made a slit down the dead deer's skin. The pounding came closer, and the air was suddenly fogged with the breath of horses ridden hard.

"What goes on here? Who killed the king's deer?" the Bishop of Hereford roared. The bishop's hands were gloved, but it was as if Marian could see through the leather to that twinkling sapphire. She gritted her teeth and more tightly gripped the knife with which she had just begun to dress the deer.

"Is it the king's deer or the prince's?" Robin answered cheekily.

"It is the king's," the bishop replied with a smirk. Marian did not like the smirk. Was the bishop saying that Prince John was king somehow? That Richard had died?

But Robin continued, "As you can see we are shepherds, but today we decided to hunt a bit and kill a fat deer."

"You're a brave fellow and the king shall know of your crime."

"By all means. When the king returns from the Crusades, perhaps we should ask him, then, whose deer these are."

"Oh, does he return?" The bishop sniggered. "We've just had word that Richard has been captured."

"What?" they all gasped.

The bishop's men moved forward and began to close in on the five shepherds. The air split with two sounds one right after the other—a shrill whistle from Marian and a blast from Robin's horn.

She felt a great gust as Ulysses, his red eyes blazing, hurled himself down on the first of the bishop's men to draw a sword, striking him with such force that he fell from his horse. Marigold took on the rest of the bishop's men as if she were chasing larks, darting in and out and striking their heads, their sword arms, their horses' ears. Soon horses were rearing, and the bishop himself was thrown to the ground. Out from the brambles thirty men in green raced with swords raised. Marian herself had yet to draw a blade. She stood in the shadow of the oak and called to her hawks, "*Ki . . . ki . . . kuh . . . kuh griss chawap!*"

By now, most of the bishop's men had fled. The bishop himself appeared stunned.

Little John now walked up to the bishop and stooped over him. "What do we do with this churchman?" he said, turning to Robin. "Off with his head?"

"Perhaps his finger," Marian said, joining Little John.

"My finger?" The bishop looked up in a daze at the

slight lad with just a trace of a mustache.

"Well, you can save your finger if you gave me your ring."

"My ring? You want my bishop's ring?"

"No, I want the Star of Jerusalem," Marian's voice had turned deadly. "Do not delay or my hawks will have your finger *and* your eyes."

The bishop tore off his glove. Marian watched as he took the ring from his finger. In the drear wintry day the star glimmered in its field of sapphire. Marian slipped the ring on her finger, then turned to Robin. "He has taken the lure. We have flown to the fist. And now it is time for his reward."

Robin brought her a hunk of the meat he had just cut from the deer. Marian held the bloody piece in her hand and offered it to the bishop. He looked at it in bewilderment. "Take it. This is the justice of falconry."

"Richard captured! I can't believe it!" Robin said. They had gathered in the blasted oak. Friar Tuck had been waiting for them. He had already heard the news from one of his most reliable sources—the chief steward's horse groom.

"Yes, they say that his ship was wrecked in the

Adriatic, near the town of Aquileia. Richard and his party were then forced to take a dangerous land route. He was trying to get to France, of course, to his mother's, Queen Eleanor's, territory."

"Who captured him?" Marian asked.

"Allies of Prince John," Friar Tuck said. "Duke Leopold of Austria. Although Richard was traveling in disguise, he was recognized." Marian touched the remnant of her mustache lightly. Had she been recognized as a girl? Robin had said that she had been foolish to talk to the bishop, for although she might, in the shadows of the shepherd's hood, give the impression of a boy, her voice gave her away. "He's being held for ransom. A large ransom to the highest bidder. So large that Queen Eleanor herself cannot afford it."

"What do we do now?" Rich asked.

"Get the gobbets," Little John said.

Friar Tuck sighed deeply. A pained expression crossed his face. "I am not sure that even those rubies will be quite enough, precious as they are."

Marian stepped forward and touched the friar's sleeve. "But the rubies and the Star of Jerusalem?" she whispered. She removed the ring from her finger.

"Yes, Marian, that would indeed ransom a king."

Chapter 25

MARKET DAY

*A hawk's beak can become too long and too sharp by
not eating enough tough food or not cracking sufficient
numbers of bones of game when it is fed. If this occurs,
the beak needs to be pared.*

I T WAS MARKET DAY in the town nearby the Fitzwalter
castle. Marian stood in a throng of people. She
had been half hoping to find Scarlet juggling, as
he often came here on market days. She was dressed
as a boy, but this time wore no mustache, and she was
listening to a minstrel who was entertaining a crowd
of mothers and children. The minstrel sang:

"Others they may tell you of bold Robin
Hood,

Derry, derry, down!
Or else of the barons bold,
But I'll tell you how they served the
        bishop,
When they robbed him of his gold.
Derry down! Hey! Derry, derry, down!"

It had only been a bit over a fortnight since the robbery of the bishop, but already the tale was being recounted in song. Part of her was, of course, relieved to hear no mention of the young lad who had actually taken the bishop's ring. *But why does Robin get all the credit?*

Marian knew it was better they did not speak of her. Robin himself had grown so worried that the bishop might have become suspicious that he had insisted she lie low until he figured out how to get the ransom of five rubies and the Star of Jerusalem to the Continent.

Marian began to notice that the people seemed to have a bit more money to spend. A woman had just handed over a coin to buy some pynade—pine nut brittle—for her children. Marian could not remember the last time she had seen anyone buying sweets for a child at market day. Indeed, she could not remember the last time she had seen a sweet seller.

When the minstrel finished the song, Marian approached the woman who had bought the pynade.

"Robin Hood?" she asked. "Who is this Robin Hood?"

"He's the reason I have money to buy a fowl." She held up a guinea hen by its legs. "And some left over to buy my children a piece of pynade. There be a reward on him by order of the sheriff now."

"Oh, no!"

"Oh, don't worry. He and his band always get away. Clever lads all of them."

Lads, Marian thought. *What about me?*

Marian made up her mind right then that she had had enough of lying low. She would seek out the boys. She had some pennies in her pocket, enough to buy a laying hen for Meg and then some left over to give to a cart driver on his way to Nottingham in exchange for a ride.

She haggled with a poulterer and managed to bargain him down a little for a hen. She also bought a bag of flour and went to the section of the village known as shambles where the butchers traded and got some kidneys for supper. Then, tucking the hen under her arm and her other bundles in a sack slung over her shoulder, she raced the two miles back to the castle.

"I'm going to find Fynn!" she announced as she ran into the castle and handed over the bird. To Meg, Robin was still Fynn and she knew nothing of Matty as Marian. She had been reluctant to tell Meg everything she had been up to in her frequent absences. She felt that if Meg knew too much it might endanger her in some way. But the old servant narrowed her eyes and looked hard at the young woman she had helped to raise. "There's more to all this, isn't there?" Her face seemed to crumple and her eyes filled with tears. "Are you going away for good, Matty? Are you never coming back?"

"No, no, Meg. I promise I'll come back. But I—I . . . have to . . . Oh, Meg, this is so hard." Now she was almost crying. She could not lie anymore. "Do you know that they call Fynn Robin now?"

Meg blinked. "So he is Robin Hood. It's as I guessed." She pressed her lips into a thin line.

"He's famous, Meg."

"And you want to be famous, too, I suppose."

Marian looked down and felt the color creeping up. "I—I . . . I don't think it's that I want to be famous, Meg. But I want to be part of something. Part of something important. Part of something that can change our country, how we live. Don't you understand?"

"I'm an old lady now," Meg said in a frail voice, "too old to understand such things perhaps."

"But didn't you have dreams when you were young?" Marian asked.

Meg's eyes misted over, then she looked over at Hodge who sat silently in the corner. His hands plucked at the hauberk. He no longer had the wits to even mend it. When Meg looked back at the girl she knew as Matty, she had tears in her eyes. "You go along. I'll try and look after your birds as best I can till you get back."

Marian embraced her tenderly. "I love you, Meg."

"I love you, too, Matty."

Chapter 26

TO SHERWOOD

By "quality of flight" it is meant that a hawk achieves altitude with minimum effort, negotiates uneven air skillfully, and sustains a glide despite wind variations. A well-trained hawk can not only perform with quality of flight but with cunning, adapting to a range of circumstances, often unexpected ones.

"AND THAT, SON," SAID the cart driver over his shoulder to Marian, who still wore her boy's leggings and tunic, "is what we folks 'round here call the Bishop's Tree." He nodded at a large oak at the next bend in the road. They were heading south.

"And why is that?"

"It be where Robin Hood done robbed the Bishop of Hereford."

Marian tried to sound surprised. "He stole money from a bishop?"

"Yes, indeed. And some say a ring as well. Quite a lad, he and his merry fellows. They don't keep nought for themselves. They gives it to the poor. And not just money, but they say that Robin be one of the best archers in all England and he takes deer regularly from the royal forests and finds a way to get it to the people. A fortnight ago, my wife and me enjoyed our first venison in over four years."

"My! And what thinks the sheriff of all this?"

"Hah! He done put a bounty on him. But the sheriff will never catch him. Robin and his lads are too clever." The cart driver paused and then in a somewhat more reflective tone continued. "They say that desperate times breed desperate men. But you know, I think it is the sheriff and that bully Sir Guy of Gisborne who are the desperate ones. From what I hear, Robin and his band never seem desperate. Even when they're robbing the rich, they joke and make merry."

Marian smiled but remained quiet.

They went on for a good while and then came to a fork in the road.

"Well," said the driver, "I fear 'tis time to part

company, lad. But 'tis not so far to Nottingham. You watch out for the sheriff's foresters and don't go poaching no deer. Leave that to the likes of Robin Hood."

"I carry only my merlin, sir," Marian said, and looked at Marigold, who perched on her shoulder.

"A pretty bird she is, too. But mind you do not set her to hunt in these parts either. They'd as soon shoot her down as anything else. It's a time of tyrants, you know. They'd put an arrow through a baby if they thought they could shake gold out of it."

"Thank you." She reached into her pocket for a few pennies.

"Keep your money, son."

"Thank you again."

She bade the cart driver farewell and set off toward Nottingham. Soon she encountered the fringes of the great woodlands of Sherwood Forest. Then she heard the rushing of the creek that was not far from the blasted oak. The rush of the creek grew louder with each step. As she broke out of a thicket and reached the bank, she gasped. The water was high and furious. How would she ever cross it without drowning? She did know how to stay afloat—she had learned from the boys—but this looked dangerous. It was the end of winter and, of course, with the melting snows the water would be high. She should have thought of this before.

Just then the roar was broken by a very loud crack. She felt Marigold tense on her shoulder. Something was crashing through the woods. A boar? A forest warden? Matty quickly crouched behind an immense rotting tree stump. The sound came closer, and with it a song. Not just a song. A hymn.

> "Sing loud the conflict, O my tongue,
> The victory that repaired our loss;
> Exalt the triumph of thy song
> To the bright trophy of the cross;
> Tell how the Lord laid down his life
> To conquer in the glorious strife."

It was Friar Tuck! He was about to wade across the creek. "Tuck!" she cried, and bounded out of the bushes. "Carry me across, will you!"

"Marian, what are you doing here? I thought you were to lie low until we got . . . er . . . certain things figured out—the gobbets and all."

"Yes, and all! The 'all,' if you remember, is largely my doing."

"Oh, of course, my dear. I don't doubt you."

"So don't you think I should be in on the planning?"

"And to that end I am to be your beast of burden and carry you across these raging waters, I suppose?" One eyebrow arched like a leaping minnow.

"I am not a burden. I weigh but eight stone. And you are no beast."

Friar Tuck sighed deeply. "How can I resist such honeyed words? Of course, my dear. Hop on my back." Marian did just that.

"And, Tuck, one thing. Perhaps 'tis better not to call me 'my dear' when I am in the clothes of a lad."

The friar cautiously dipped his sandaled left foot into the creek, and continued until the water was above his knees. "Ooooo!! Freezing my backside and my front side and everything in between!" he yelped. The waters swirled around him, and the skirts of his cassock spread out like a rumpled lily pad, but he continued to make his way through the boisterous waters as if he were walking across a pond on a windless summer day.

They had just reached the midpoint of the creek when Robin appeared from behind a screen of alders on the opposite side.

"I told you to lie low," he called to Marian, then turned and raised his horn to blow. A shaft of sunlight fell upon him and Marian felt her heart race. It seemed as if Robin had grown taller even in the brief time since she had last seen him. His hair brushed his shoulder in burnished curls, and his cheeks bristled with the stubble the same color as the hair she had spotted on his chest that day she had tried to fix his cloak. From his belt hung a good broadsword of well-tempered steel. He was a gallant sight. She had to admit she was very glad that today she was not wearing a false mustache.

As Friar Tuck set her down, the others came out of the woods. It was a strange moment, for here she was, looking like a boy with her shorn hair and dressed in leggings, and yet the boys she knew had become men.

"Now, Friar Tuck, I didn't know you were a fisherman," Robin said.

"Well, I do believe I fished up a fine lass and not a fish, Robin."

Chapter 27

THE BLASTED OAK

Derris dust, a compound made from the roots of the derris plant, is effective in treating feather lice.

FRIAR TUCK, MARIAN, AND Robin made their way back to the blasted oak. Marian stood up in the charred hollow. There was tension in the air. She looked at the others—Rich, Scarlet, Little John. And then everyone turned their gaze expectantly toward Friar Tuck. The jolly demeanor he had displayed earlier as he and Marian crossed the creek had vanished. His face was somber.

"What is it? Have they killed King Richard?" she asked.

Robin looked at the friar. The monk shook his head. "No, no. Nothing that bad. At least not yet. But they now know the rubies are missing."

"But how?"

"I am sorry to say that the first thing that the abbess did was to go to that creek bank in Barnsdale and look for them. She found them missing."

"How do you know all this?"

"I have my ways. A man of the cloth hears many things both in confession and out. Of course, now the prince, the sheriff, Gisborne, and the whole lot of them are worried for precisely the reasons they should be— that someone will use them to ransom the king. They wanted to use the rubies instead to bribe someone to murder Richard."

"In other words, it's a race," Marian said succinctly.

"Truly a race between us and them to get the rubies and the Star of Jerusalem into the right hands," Friar Tuck said gravely.

"We should get them now. And deliver them as quickly as possible," Marian said.

"Easier said than done," Robin replied. "Those forests are heavily patrolled, more so than when we first hid the gobbets."

There was a moment of silence, and then Marian said, "But don't you see, I might be able to use my hawks to retrieve them."

"Brilliant!" Rich said. "Absolutely brilliant!"

"Marian, that is the perfect solution. And when the birds get them, you can tell them to bring them here. You can do that, can't you?" Robin spoke with mounting excitement. "And then we can leave immediately for the Continent."

It was something in the way Robin said "we" that set off a small alarm in Marian's head. "We? You mean me as well?" The boys exchanged nervous glances. A deep frown creased her brow. "You mean I'm not going with you?"

"Of course you're not going with us," Robin said, almost crossly.

"What do you mean 'of course'?" She felt her temper rising. "Why am I to be excluded?" Robin started to speak, but Marian interrupted. "I'm sick of being left out, left behind. I'm sick of this stupid country and this stupid prince! I'm not just a girl anymore. You have to understand that."

Robin looked startled. The saddest part was that she had thought Robin *did* understand. She recalled not just his words when she had come up with the plan for taking the ring from the bishop but the look in his eyes. That gaze of profound respect as he had said "She knows her business. We do as Marian says." How could things change so quickly?

"You were never *just* a girl," Robin said. His eyes, deep blue like twin seas, seemed to engulf her. "But now you are a woman."

They all looked at one another. No one knew what to say.

"She's right," Robin said, breaking the silence. "She's our strategist. It was Marian after all who devised the plan for robbing the bishop. Without the Star of Jerusalem we would not have enough ransom to speak of, and, needless to say, without her we wouldn't have the rubies either."

Marian could not help but wonder if he was recalling that time years before when they had cut her out of the tree house building scheme, and Robin had come to apologize for his "beastly" behavior.

A welter of emotions boiled up within Marian. Her eyes met Robin's, and she saw not just his trust but something more. An overwhelming joy swept through her entire being. *He loves me and I love him. I love him!* She almost reeled. *I would die for him, but I will not stay back for him . . . and he no longer wants me to.*

Chapter 28

WATCHED

The healthy hawk flies with an unmatched buoyancy
through the air. She can fly on a slant, level, or straight
up. The fast flier never flies steadily or at the same rate.
She is constantly adjusting for minute wind changes—
this, too, is considered quality of flight.

BY THE NEXT EVENING Marian had returned to the castle and realized that it did not make sense to use all her hawks to retrieve the jewels. It would only complicate matters, not to mention that five hawks would attract more attention than one. Now that Moss was so feeble, Marigold was the obvious choice. Not only did she and Marian communicate easily but also she was the smallest. If there were royal foresters around she would be the least noticeable.

It did not take Marian long to make her way with Marigold the mile or so down the road and then to cut across the dark field to the edge of the forest. She was not sure when she began having an uneasy feeling, but she hesitated to leave the field. The greenwood of Barnsdale was not nearly as dense as that of Sherwood. The pathways were not as tangled. It was easier for a royal forester to find a poacher, and, although she had not seen any signs of a forester, she was wary. It was as if some sixth sense were telling her not to go farther but rather to wait, to watch. She had the peculiar feeling that she was being watched. Had someone followed her? She crouched beside a large rock.

As time passed she became more uneasy. Marigold refused to leave her shoulder. This was not like the merlin, who would often scout ahead for Marian. This evening she huddled close to her mistress and even tried to tuck herself into the hood of Marian's cloak. *I can't move,* Marian thought. *It's too dangerous to move.*

Marian looked up through the dark embroidery of the trees and watched as the stars transcribed the sky. She was thankful that it was a moonless night, for all she sought was darkness and shadow. The first tree with a ruby was no more than a short walk from where she crouched. But she could not move. She imagined the jewel's flickering red light smothered by the mosses they had wrapped it in, deep in the hole of the deserted nest of the sparrow hawk. It beckoned her, glimmering in her brain. But she could not move.

Her heart slowed. She closed her eyes. *I cannot go. I must not move.* And yet she could not let herself fall asleep. She tried to remember the look in Robin's eyes when he had said that she was a woman and their strategist. There had been something there that went beyond simply trusting her, and at the time she had felt it was love. But what if she was wrong? She tried hard to remember his expression when he'd spoken, but somehow it became harder and harder to summon up his face. *Oh dear . . . does he even think about me . . . ever? When I am not around does* he *try to imagine* my *face?*

She stayed crouching in the shadow of the rock until the darkness thinned to a frayed gray dawn. If there had been someone watching, she had sensed him but never actually heard him. She had wondered as dawn approached if she should have taken a chance and directed Marigold to fetch at least one of the rubies. But Marigold had remained as nervous as her mistress through the long night.

Now Marian heard horses. It was the morning guard of the foresters. She really had to get out before they found her. The distance across the field to the road was less than a quarter of a mile. If she could make it to the road, she could be any young person on her way to the village on an errand.

She crept from her hiding place and then scrambled through the tall grass on her belly until she finally made it to the road, where she stood and began to walk. Marigold at last regained her boldness and flew a short distance ahead as they walked toward the castle, darting back to signal that the way was clear.

Marian did not go back into the woods that day, nor the next night nor the next. She had Meg take a basket of eggs from their one laying hen to sell at the market with a coded message for Friar Tuck. It had been arranged that he would frequent some of their old code-exchange places as often as he could. In the message she said that she felt she was being watched. She was amazed when, within the space of two days, a message was returned. Deciphering it, she read, *You are, as am I. Be careful.*

Marian realized it was going to be impossible to

go to the woods herself. Yet this was not like jessless hawking, for the prey was entirely different—not hares or ducks but rubies! She racked her brains to think of a way she could tell the hawks not only the oddity of the "prey" but exactly which trees contained the rubies. Even if she could communicate this information, she was hesitant to send Marigold, Morgana, Lyra, or Ulysses out unaccompanied. All hawks had a certain degree of superstition. What would Moss and the others think when she told them about rubies hidden in trees called the lepers of the forest, where the diseased sparrow hawks had lived? She began slowly.

"Hechmon dwasch quinx keenash . . ." (Indeed. There are five abandoned tree hollows in the greenwood of Barnsdale and in their hollows I have buried a king's ransom—five rubies.)

"The nests were abandoned because the sparrow hawks got the tick disease—weren't they, Matty?" Lyra said quietly. To her hawks she would always be Matty.

"Yes. I would never lie to you. If you don't want to go, I understand."

Moss now spoke. "It's an old hawk's tale that you can get this disease from just being in a tree where a sick sparrow hawk had lived. I will go." Marian closed her eyes, grateful that the dear old bird had so quickly agreed. But Moss was the most enfeebled of her hawks, the one least likely to be able to help.

"I hope you never doubted that I would go, Matty," Marigold said.

"And I, too, will go," Ulysses snapped.

"Count me in," said Morgana.

"And me," said Lyra.

Marian looked at her hawks through the scrim of tears. *Do birds cry?* Marian wondered. "You are all so good. You are the noblest of birds, and because of you we shall bring back King Richard the Lionheart, the noblest of rulers. Now let me try and explain where the trees are." The birds exchanged nervous looks. Marian was not sure why. Perhaps they were having second thoughts.

"Pschwap muchta tawba tawba y greicha . . ." (You go due west, then angle south by southeast when you get to the forest. There is a sycamore and a grove of birches. . . .) Talking softly she tried to trace out the location of the trees with the rubies for the birds now gathered around her in the mews.

Lyra alighted on the floor next to Marian, who was

scratching a diagram on the stones with a charred stick. "The problem is that this is not how hawks navigate," Lyra said. "Words . . . words . . . pictures . . ." As Lyra tried to explain, Marian realized that although she had mastered the language of the hawks, she still needed to learn the way her hawks navigated. It had nothing to do with words and even less with flat drawing.

Moss's voice was thin and cracked. "You see, dear, it is especially hard within the stone walls of this tower to explain our ways of getting from place to place. Though I can barely see anymore, when I am outside I can feel. I can feel the location of the stars, the pull of the sun and the moon, the earth points."

"The earth points?" Marian asked.

"It's difficult to explain. But there are two *places* on this earth—opposite each other—that help us. Our brains are very sensitive to the one we call *nwamelk*."

"*Nwamelk*," Marian repeated. This word was unfamiliar to her.

"*Nwamelk*—it is a combination of two words, really, *north* and *pull*."

"You mean you are pulled north?"

"Not exactly . . ." Moss scratched one talon on the floor in frustration as if looking for an answer. "It is a way of thinking, a manner in which our minds and not just our eyes guide us. Humans have maps. This is like a map in our brains, but it is not flat. That is the problem with what you draw here with your stick. The lines are flat. It has no shape for us."

"So it's hopeless." Marian sighed.

"No!" Marigold suddenly spoke up. "If I could go, I could get a bearing on one tree, and then I could guide the others."

"You mean you could tell them?"

The hawks looked at one another. Their Matty was as much like a bird as a human being could be, but she didn't understand that "tell" was not how *nwamelk* worked.

"Not tell, Matty." Hearing her old name brought Marian back to a strange moment years before, that day when she had come back tired and happy after Marigold's first free flight. Was that the first time when she had felt herself cross over the invisible border between human and hawk? Then she remembered another early instance. She had gone to bed but could not sleep and began to experience a peculiar state that was more like a trance than a dream in which she found herself separating from and seemingly perched above her own body. She had sensed a curious stirring in her shoulders and at the same time her vision had become unimaginably sharp. She had seen with an absolute clarity. And now she remembered another part of that odd time. She had in fact felt a faint pull in her head as if she knew for the first time exactly where she was, not just in her castle, not just in her shire, not just in England but on Earth! Perhaps this was what the hawks meant when they told her about *nwamelk*.

If only she could get Marigold to that first tree! Marian knew she would have to go with her merlin. There was no other way. But there were eyes out there. Eyes watching.

Chapter 29

TRAPPED!

The early signs of a hawk in a poor or low condition
are often difficult to read. "Slitted eyes" can be very
ambiguous, as they can indicate contentment as well
as a digestive problem. If your bird refuses to eat,
feed it sugared water and leave the hawk in a
dark place for an hour.

IT HAD BEEN NEARLY three months since the news of King Richard's capture. He was still alive, and so far no one had come up with money to ransom his life and freedom or to pay for his murder. But finally it was mid-March when the worst storms happen, as if winter is trying to have the last word. The wind howled and the night turned white with snow. The snow changed to sleet and the slashing wet wind drove the sleet slantwise across the night. Branches torn from trees sailed through the air.

Surely no one will be out on a night like this. And no one can see me if they are out, Marian thought as she made her way toward the greenwood with Marigold flying a short distance ahead. The merlin, who had no problem plowing through the wild gusts, circled back frequently to keep in sight of her mistress. "*Mwup wup* . . . I'm coming . . . I'm coming," Marian muttered and thought again as she had so many times before, *Would that I had wings!*

At last they were at the edge of the forest and making their way toward the first of the trees. "*Hwatz kruschick.*" Marigold settled on her shoulder and Marian began to speak to her. She knew that words were no good for a hawk's navigation, but she could still describe the tree if, God willing, the wind had not torn it down and Marigold would see that it was a different kind of tree. It was Marian's notion that once Marigold had seen one of these forest lepers she'd recognize the others.

"*Frymchisch, amrigod, frym chisch* . . ." (See it yonder. Even on this foul night it looks strange, doesn't it?) Marian said, spotting the tree several yards ahead.

"*Hagge hagge,*" Marigold replied. Marian felt delight course through her. The merlin understood. She saw. This was no drawing, no flat lines. Then a shrill cry cracked the air.

Marian felt the merlin flee from her shoulder as she herself dropped. The drop was not long and the landing not hard, but she heard a sickening snap over her head.

She was momentarily stunned. Then she screamed. "*Cranaggg, Marigold!* Flee, Marigold! I've been trapped!" Snared by a net, she'd been dropped into a cage of woven wattle. She felt something tight around her ankles. They had put jesses on her! She must have stepped into the loops and that was what had triggered the trap to open and snare her. It was too late. The locks and swivels of the jesses were beyond her reach. She closed her eyes. And uttered a prayer in a language no human had ever heard. "*Gyllman ichtio, Marigold leschen me, leschen me gwap.*"

Chapter 30

THE NEVER-ENDING NIGHT

Bating is a headlong dive of rage and terror by which a leashed falcon leaps from a fist in a bid for freedom. If not handled correctly, the bird can do permanent damage to its flight feathers, the primaries in particular.

THE TRAP WAS LARGE; large enough for a deer but fashioned like a wattle cage for a bird, a big bird with a large wingspan.

The wind had died down, and Marian heard first the footsteps and then the voices. She had not been in the trap long. She wondered if they had put traps everywhere in the woods. How long had they been waiting for her? Or was it her? Perhaps they'd been hunting someone else? Once she and the boys had built their tree houses throughout this same greenwood to watch for the prince's and the sheriff's men, and now with a ground trap they had snared her.

"She'll be happy. This will earn us a nice fat pig."

Marian knew immediately who they were talking about. There was only one "she" who would be happy with this bird being captured: the abbess.

A heavy cloth was thrown over the cage before Marian could see her captors. There was a jerk and she felt herself being raised. They began to walk with the cage and continued walking longer than it had taken her to walk from the edge of the forest to where she had been trapped. But she now heard another voice and the snort of some horses.

"You got her?" the new voice asked.

"We got her."

"I don't hear anything. Sure she's alive?"

"This trap ain't going to kill anything. But I'll check."

She was set down. The cloth was pulled back and a bloodshot watery blue eye peered down into the cage. "Missy, you all right in there, ain't you? Won't be long now."

"Mweep phrynghiss bletchmig," she muttered.

"Whatcha say there?"

"Mweep phrynghiss bletchmig," Marian repeated. She was not sure why these old hawk curses that she had learned in the mews came back to her. She knew how to curse in English but only hawk came out.

"I think her brains done been addled. But she looks all right." He threw the cover back over the cage.

She felt herself being lifted and set down again. But this time not on the ground. She could tell by the sound that there were planks beneath her. She guessed they'd put her in a cart and soon she heard the creak of the wheel. The cart lurched forward. Her heart raced. She had to think of something. *Would Marigold have flown back to tell the others? Of course. She must have. No, maybe she would have stayed to see where they were taking me.*

The trip seemed endless. She drifted off to sleep for short periods of time, but then she awoke and felt the jesses around her ankles and a fury started to rise in her. She tried to calm herself. Hawks could not hunt when they were in a fret. She really had to think like a hawk now. But she was not the hunter, she was the hunted. Not the predator but the prey. The cart jolted to a halt and panic swept through her. Once more she felt the cage being lifted and carried for a short distance. A heavy door was opened and a low voice wormed through the darkness. "Put it down."

She felt a bump as the cage was dropped to the floor. Then there was the sound of feet retreating, a heavy door creaking shut, and finally silence. But she knew she was not alone.

She heard a heavy tread on the floorboards, a sigh, and the groaning sag of a chair as someone sat down. She could feel the awful transparent eyes piercing the cloth that covered her cage. Her heart roared in her chest. Never had she felt such tumult, such anger. A mixture of terror and defiance welled up inside her, and Marian lurched madly. There was a sharp yank on the jesses that cut through her thick stockings. She yelped. There was another violent jerk that twisted her leg painfully. Pain shot up her calf all the way to her hip. The awful presence moved closer.

"I demand to be let out!" she shouted with all the dignity she could muster. And then she heard a harsh laugh and felt a sharp poke from a stick.

"Shut up!" A woman's voice seared the air.

"What is this about? I demand to know!"

"*You* demand? You *demand*?" The voice was scalding. Suddenly the cloth was removed. A scaly hand reached between the bars of the cage and grabbed her just under the jaw. The fingers dug into the skin of her cheek. She gasped as she looked up. What she saw looked more like a mask than a human face. There was a waxen shininess, as if the face had melted. But no matter, the eyes had remained the same, two transluscent voids. The lipless mouth was a smear across the face. *I did that,* Matty thought. And the memory of that shriek she had heard when she had knocked over the candle rang clearly in her ears. *I did this to her and now she will take her vengeance.*

The abbess's voice remained low and calm but full of strange heat.

"I understand you are a falconer, milady. I understand that the first stage in the training of a hawk is called manning him, or her, as it is."

Hearing those words, something hardened in Marian. She would not let this woman frighten her. She lifted her chin and looked straight at her tormentor with dark insolence.

The abbess sniffed and averted her eyes but continued speaking. "I understand that the bird is never left alone, that the trainer shall make the falcon accustomed to him—or her." She gave a dry little laugh. "Furthermore, the creature remains hooded at all times until it is completely within the power of the trainer. Godfrey!" She called out sharply. Marian heard the door open.

"Yes, Abbess."

"The hood!"

In the moment when they hooded her, Marian recognized the abbess's fatal error in what was to be her training. For she tasted her own blood. The blood that trickled down her cheek where the abbess's nails had dug into her skin was proof to her that she would never be brought within the abbess's absolute power. The art of true falconry—teaching with patience and respect—called for the falconer to hold the bird firmly and gently so it would not be injured.

Through the shadowy days and nights that followed, it was this taste of her own blood that sustained her determination to never succumb to the power of the abbess. She would never be tamed.

The hood they placed on Marian was of dark stiff leather, with a slit through which they fed her. Their intention was to keep her awake, yet deprived of vision. Thus they'd wear down her resistance so that after days, she would be so starved for light and so desperate to see the world that finally, like a falcon, she would capitulate and climb willingly and lovingly on to the "falconer's" glove and reveal the location of the rubies. But, in fact, the abbess had grown soft over the years with the wines and rich meats the sheriff and the prince had provided in exchange for many of the abbey's treasures and she could not stay awake herself. Marian realized this shortly into the first night when the abbess yawned loudly and ordered another sister to come in and watch her. Soon that sister was also asleep, snoring softly through the night. So it was no problem for Marian to sleep in brief snatches and generally keep her strength up. She would never climb on to the perch, the promise of being unhooded and set free that the abbess held out in exchange for the secret of the rubies' whereabouts.

The abbess's strategy for extracting this information was crude, but she'd begun that first evening. "There is a way, my dear, that we can shorten your training considerably. I shall let you ponder it, but first you need to know that *we* know that you are not simply Matilda Fitzwalter, daughter of the late Lord William, who fought in England first for King Henry and then for his son Richard in France, but you have several other identities as well. You are, of course, the clumsy serving girl, one Marian Greenleaf. You were at one point also known as the Nut Brown Girl by some, for you played with a certain Robert Woodfynn and Hubert Bigge and others in the greenwood and turned brown from the sun. Robert, of course, became Robin Hood and now leads his Merry Men including Hubert Bigge, now called Little John. There is one young maiden, Maid Marian, I understand, who sometimes disguises herself as a boy. An adolescent boy who has but a trace of a mustache but who nonetheless stole a ring from the Bishop of Hereford's finger."

"It was my mother's jewel!" Marian shot back.

"There are other jewels that concern me."

"I don't know what you're talking about."

"Yes, you do. Don't be fresh with me, girl. For years you and that gang have been spotted in and about the Barnsdale forest, especially down by the creek. I am talking about the rubies. Where are they?"

"I don't know!"

"How could you *not* know? You little liar." There was a phlegmy sound and something hit the hood.

"You spat on me!"

"I'll do worse." There was a sharp yank on the jesses,

and Marian screamed with pain.

"You spat on me, you draw my blood, and yet you think you will tame me? Woman, you know nothing about falconry."

"But I know about pain and how it can loosen tongues."

"And you think you can get the truth through torture? Why would I not say anything—tell any lie to stop pain?" She heard the abbess inhale sharply and then get up to leave.

But each day the abbess returned to ask where the gems were hidden, and each day Marian said nothing. She had been kept hooded, and her ankles were raw and bleeding from the rope burns of the jesses, yet she still refused to be tamed. She sat erect in the middle of the cell, tethered to a ring in the floor by a chain attached to the jesses, her head held high and defiant. The training was most definitely not proceeding on schedule. Marian did not seem tired and she would not bate. As each day slipped into dusk and dusk to night and one night into another, Marian sensed the abbess's growing panic to find the jewels.

One day she heard the abbess enter the cell, sit down heavily in the chair, and sigh. Marian lifted her hooded head a bit higher. "You are a very proud girl. Too proud," the abbess observed. "But," she continued, "you are a girl, not a bird. That perhaps has been my error." Marian did not deign to reply. Just then the sound of a leper's bell could be heard.

"Ah!" exclaimed the abbess and clapped her hands gleefully. "You know of course we have a leprosarium attached to the abbey? The sound of a leper's bell signals a new arrival."

Marian did not respond, but the abbess spoke with a new energy. "My work in this hospital has been widely praised. Even the pope has written to the Bishop of Hereford commending me. I believe the letter said that the hospital of this abbey offers 'a matchless spiritual blessing for the region.'" She paused as if to reflect. "Yes, those were his exact words. I had a special chantry built, and the lepers are required to spend several hours each day praying for the souls of their benefactors. So not only have I provided for the health of those afflicted with leprosy but at the same time I have provided for the health of my own soul."

"Through forced prayer—hah!" Marian laughed scornfully.

"Oh, you're laughing, are you? Well, perhaps you

need to take a closer look at this hospital and in doing so—who knows, Maid Marian, you might provide for the health of *your* soul."

Marian turned her head. Despite the hood she felt as if she were staring directly into those terrible eyes, set like pale lifeless stones. "I would rather burn in hell than share one moment in any heaven that would welcome you."

There was a long silence, then Marian felt her head being wrenched around.

"Don't toy with me, girl!" The abbess's fingers dug into her neck. "I do believe it is time to unhood you!"

"Is it?" Marian replied quietly.

"Yes. A funeral for the living dead is about to commence. I have new plans for you and your 'training.'" She ripped off Marian's hood. Marian blinked in the dim dawn light. The abbess's translucent eyes shimmered with a fiendish gleam.

Chapter 31

THE LIVING DEAD

The last sanctuary, inviolable, incorruptible for the abused hawk, is death. Many a mishandled bird has chosen to die.

THE ABBESS DRAGGED MARIAN to a window. Marian's eyes closed at the sudden glint of the rising sun as it reflected off a silver cross borne by a priest on the road below. Behind the priest was a small procession winding up the road to the abbey.

"You see!" rasped the abbess, pointing to a pathetic creature at the end of the procession, "There she is. Face eaten away, one foot half gone."

Head bowed, her frail body supported by a crutch, the leper moved slowly. Strapped to her back were two wood planks and a bag of nails for the coffin she would be required to build soon after she entered the abbey hospital. Apparently she didn't have the strength to carry any more than this, for the rest of the planks were carried by men in the procession.

"And now to the chantry!" announced the abbess almost gaily.

In the chantry, no one stood close to the creature. A black cloth had been draped over two trestles in front of the altar where the leper knelt to hear Mass and make her last confession. The arrangement of the cloth and the trestles looked precisely like a funeral bier upon which a coffin would be set.

The priest was an elderly man, whose voice was weak and barely audible as he chanted, "Libera me, Domine." It was a chant for the dead, for a departed soul, and yet the woman lived.

The service was not long. When it concluded, the leper limped to the door of the church from which she would be led to the hospital. Before she left the church, the priest at the door signaled her to stop. Marian felt herself break into a cold sweat when she saw the priest stoop, reach into a bucket and pour some earth over the woman's remaining whole foot, as one would pour dirt onto a coffin in an open grave. Muttering in Latin, the priest then spoke his final words to the leper: *"Tu eres morte ad vivendi pero vivendi ad Domine.* Thou art dead to the living but alive again for God." He tied a black ribbon on to the leper's crutch.

The abbess leaned close to Marian and whispered, "The ribbon is the gravestone. We don't waste time or money with real stones. But it does have a little prayer stitched on it. The nuns do the needlework." She smiled grimly, then continued to speak. "We have been most successful in routing out lepers. I shall be blessed for this, you know." She paused. Her hand gripped hard on Marian's arm. "And so shall you."

"Me?"

"Yes, you. We need someone to tend them. They are getting so ill, this batch, that they cannot do their fair share of praying—praying for the souls of those like me who provide them this beneficence."

As Marian entered the hospital room, she felt that the priest might as well have sprinkled earth on her own feet. It was as if she were stepping into a coffin—a coffin of the living And this was where she was supposed to stay. The most horribly deformed bodies lay in heaps before her, puddles of disintegrating flesh and bones.

Their voices muttered oaths and prayers. Their breath whistled through the craggy remnants of their faces. Marian scanned the room for the leper who had just arrived. Then in the shadows she saw the crutch with the black ribbon on the floor and near it a pile of rags. The rags seemed to have no form. If there had been a body, it must have simply dissolved. Had the poor creature died and been spirited away to heaven?

But then from the pile a voice scratched the air, so dim it sounded no louder than the tiny claws of mice on stone. But something drew Marian to that heap.

Despite the filth, the tattered shreds of skin, the rankness of the odor that rose like a putrid mist as Marian drew nearer, she also felt a pureness of spirit. A stream of light and blessedness flowed from the moldering heap of flesh. This time she did not make the mistake she had years before on that moonlit night on the road to the greenwood. Marian knelt and bowed her head. "Milady Helena, how might I serve you?"

"Good child, I am so happy to see you." The leper sighed deeply. "If only Robin Hood knew where you are."

"Robin Hood! You know Robin Hood?" Marian was dumbfounded.

"Oh, my dear, of course I do. Old friends, really. He tried to help me just like his mum. You know his mother, Nelly Woodfynn, always helped me when she could. When I first met you on that road, I was on my way to Nelly's. But then Barnsdale became too dangerous for lepers and I found my way elsewhere. 'Twas only perhaps a fortnight ago that I met Robin again. He knew me from my coming to his mum's, and he did help me so much. Found me a refuge, brought me food, warm clothes. But he was not the same boy I remembered—carefree and always merry. Indeed none of his Merry Men seemed happy but worn down with grief. And I found out it was all for you, my dear, the one sometimes called the Nut Brown Girl. He loves you, you know, but he fears you are dead. And here you are—alive but tending the living dead!" Helena paused and sighed softly. "And now he will think I am dead, too, when he comes back to look for me. Or he'll think that the abbess has found me as she has the others." Helena gestured toward the people around her, sleeping on piles of rags in the shadowy corners of the hospital.

Marian's head was swirling. Robin knew Helena. Helena knew about Marian. Not only that, Helena knew that Robin loved her. "If only . . . if only he knew that I am alive . . . well . . . here with you."

Marian vowed that if Robin and his mother, Nelly, had taken care of Helena, so would she. She refused to be afraid of the disease.

In the days that came, she washed the woman, fed her, and helped the others. Fear, Marian decided, was a worse sickness than leprosy.

But what obsessed her day and night was how she might get a message to Robin, to let him know that she was alive and where she was. She hated to think that he imagined her dead. More than the leprosy, Marian feared that Robin thought she was dead and had stopped looking for her.

One morning Marian had been shaking the lice out of the bedclothes when she heard Helena stir behind her.

"What a lovely merlin that is outside on the branch." Helena's face—really no more than a noseless skull within a black hood—had turned toward one of the narrow slit windows in the thick stone walls.

"Merlin!" Marian ran to the window. Looking out into the abbey's orchard, in the middle of the blizzard of white apple blossoms she spotted her. "Marigold! *Tshaw pschaw chu churrrru tschaw*." The words spilled from Marian's mouth in a torrent and tears streamed down her face. Marigold flew to the window and lit on her mistress's fist. With her small tongue she began to lick the salty tears from Marian's cheeks. Marigold was here and Marian knew she could survive anything now. She might be among the living dead, but within herself she felt new life.

The next day Marigold came with Ulysses and Lyra. Soon after the kestrel Morgana appeared. "My little hawk mistress!" Marian whispered with delight as she realized that Marigold had led them here. It gave Marian great ease to know the hawks had been able to get out and fend for themselves and Meg and Hodge while she had been imprisoned.

Marian went to Helena. "Helena, my birds have come here—here to seek me out. They look well, and that they have come here for me. . . . It seems like some sort of a miracle."

"Now you must be careful that the abbess does not lay a trap for your birds," Helena replied in her thin voice. "For the miracle is that they have found you, and not only that but that the little merlin told the other hawks and—" Helena paused. Speaking required a great effort, but her next words were important and she wanted them to be clear. Swallowing hard, she continued, "If she told the others, she could tell Robin Hood."

Marian's eyes widened. Of course this was exactly what she had wanted—for Robin to know she was alive.

"So now you must send a message to Robin Hood. The little merlin, the one you call Marigold, can carry it."

"But I have no pen and ink. How can I write anything?"

"I do not think that words are needed. And I think that Robin is watching the hawks and following their flight. He needs only a sign, a sign that you are alive." She stopped to get her breath. "Send him a lock of your hair. Take the small blade we use for cutting what little food they give us and clip a lock from your hair. A bird flying with such a thing will not be noticed. It will look like stuff for a nest."

Of course, she didn't need to write anything. Marigold knew where the blasted oak was in Sherwood.

This was not like trying to explain the trees in which the rubies were hidden. She began immediately to whisper to the merlin. *"Meelpa, pischwatch.* Robin *gimmlich bruscha."* While she was speaking to Marigold, explaining what the bird was to do, she sawed away with the knife on her still rather short hair.

That evening Robin sat with his men in the hollow of the blasted oak. At first it had seemed as if Marian had simply vanished. Then, through their network of spies, they heard she had been captured. "It's just so—so odd that we have not a clue where she's been taken," Robin said, shaking his head sadly. "Does she still live? That is the worst. We know not if she is alive or dead."

"She lives. I am sure of that," Friar Tuck said. "But where? And what are they doing to her?"

Robin buried his face in his hands. They had set out to rescue a king with rubies and a sapphire, and now something far more precious to him than any jewels or any king had vanished. The men looked at one another as they saw their leader, weary with worry, shake his head and wipe tears from his eyes.

A grim silence settled upon them. In the space of that silence a merlin swooped through the leafy branches of the oak and into the vast hollow to alight on Robin's shoulder.

He looked up in shock.

"Why, it's Marigold," Little John said.

"So it is!" Scarlet rose and looked in awe at the bird.

A lock of curly hair dropped into Robin's lap. "It's Marian's," Robin said in awe. "She sent it. This is a sign. She lives!" His eyes widened in thought. "But where? How?" He turned to Marigold. The merlin cocked her head and peered with great curiosity into Robin's eyes.

Robin felt something stir inside him. It seemed peculiar and yet there was a feeling of something slightly familiar. Perhaps it was just a glimmer of the communication with birds that Marian had known all these years, but he felt that this bird might become his ally. Had not Marian often told him that for a true falconer a well-taught bird was never a captive but a partner?

Suddenly Robin knew what he should do. In his shirt, he had some hedgehog bristles and a tuft of robin's feather that he always used for fletching his arrows. There was no way that Marian would fail to recognize them as his. He quickly tied the bristles and tuft into a small bundle and placed it on his fist in the time-honored tradition.

Marigold approached the offering with all the dignity and nobility of her ancestry. She snagged the bundle in her beak, then settled on his fist. Robin walked out of the hollow with his arm extended. As he had seen Marian do countless times, he thrust his arm into the air. Marigold spread her wings; roused them once, twice; and then lifted off in flight.

Slowly she rose and circled frequently so that Robin might follow her path in the darkening day. He got onto his horse and followed her, his heart bursting with gratitude, as Marigold led them steadily toward Nottingham.

"So she is there," he said to himself as Marigold circled the abbey on the knoll three times. *And now to rescue her,* he thought. *But how?* The chief strategist of the band was a prisoner. It was up to him now.

Chapter 32

THE BEGINNING OF THE END

*If a growing hawk is insufficiently fed, the fledgling
feathers might continue to grow, but within them
there will be a telltale weak section that shows as a
slash or a streak in the full-grown plume. Such streaks
are called hunger traces and will affect the bird's
ability to fly until the next molt.*

"Y OUR DINNER, MILADY!"

Marian looked up, confused, from the
corner where she sat with Helena. The abbess
never entered the hospital, let alone bearing a plate of
food for her. Food was always shoved into the outer
chamber by a young scullery maid. But there was
the abbess, holding a plate with something red and
steaming on it.

"What?" Marian asked.

"'What,' you say? You don't recognize it? I certainly thought you would, my little hawk mistress! 'Tis the brain of a freshly slaughtered rabbit. I understand they are a favorite of predatory birds from hawks to eagles. I am told that such birds crush the rabbits' skulls with their talons, that indeed their talons are much stronger than their beaks. Here, my dear, have a crop full!" She laughed and set the plate on the floor. "Oh, and when you tire of rabbit brains perhaps your own brain will commence to work and remember the whereabouts of the rubies."

Marian pressed her hand to her rib cage where she kept the small precious bundle of feather and hedgehog bristle under her bodice. Marigold had dropped the bundle through the window that morning. Helena had been right—all that was needed was a sign. With the lock of hair and the bundle of fletching both she and Robin knew the other to be alive. She did not attempt to eat the raw bloody mess. No self-respecting raptor—be she hawk, falcon, or eagle—would ever take food from a tyrant. Refusal was her last weapon against her captor. "Robin will be here soon," she kept telling herself. "Soon." The bundle of feathers was nourishment enough. But he did not come, not that day nor the next nor the next. And still more days passed and yet there was no sign of him. Only the abbess came—sometimes with a mound of raw rabbits' brains, other times with the still-quivering heart of a guinea fowl—all the delicacies that Marian had at one time or another served her own birds. Marian refused to eat. Nor would she eat the food of the lepers despite their begging her to do so. The abbess became wary: if the girl died they would never find the rubies.

Marian was growing thinner and weaker with each day, but her gaze became haughtier, nearly murderous with contempt.

The lepers moved beyond their own despair as they saw the person who had treated them so kindly wasting away before them. One morning Marian collapsed not far from Helena's pallet. They could do nothing to make her comfortable. Helena had been begging her to eat the raw, bloody organs offered by the abbess, but Marian would only say, "He will come. Fear not."

Marian's breath grew raspy. Her eyelids barely flickered, and soon she did not respond at all. To the lepers who lived constantly within the shadows of death, who knew intimately the signs of finality, and who had witnessed so often the passing of the spirit from the body, it appeared that she was dying.

At the window Marigold perched transfixed, watching, but strangely calm. Indeed, the little merlin was experiencing a sensation that she had never known in her life. It was not hunger, nor was it the peculiar quickening she felt as she swooped to kill prey. It was a sensation close to that early exhilaration she had known on her first free flight. Something was stealing over the bird that seemed familiar but at the same time very strange. It was the spirit of her mistress.

Chapter 33

MATTY ONCE MORE!

Yarak is the state of being keen for flight. It is senseless to launch a hawk prematurely before it is in yarak. It is the fluffing rattle of the feathers being roused that is the signal that the hawk is in good humor and ready for flight.

WITHIN THE SOULS OF certain living things there is territory where humans and animals can meet and join in a perfect communion. Marian grew very still and her breathing shallower as she engaged in the greatest effort of her life. She felt something pushing in her brain, exploring hidden channels as the spirit of Marigold began to mesh with hers and her own brain sought out the recesses hidden within the maze of the bird's mind.

Then, suddenly, they were there together, the young woman and the bird. There, in a time before time, touching the spirits of all the creatures before they became separate ones. There in the time of shared memories, with the taste of the first warm salt water, the first oceans on their tongues, and the fragrance of the first forests from millions upon millions of years ago.

The scent of green flooded Matty's nostrils. She would always be Matty in yarak and never Marian, for it was as Matty that her birds knew her. She felt her own bloodstream joined with another's, and a stirring in her shoulders. She felt the mighty wings unfurl. She roused her feathers twice. A keenness streamed through her. She knew the response well. She was in yarak and ready to fly. Her wings beat as she rose on measured strokes.

Other lepers thought she had at this very instant died, but Helena looked out the window that now framed Marigold's flight as she disappeared over the orchard's trees and knew that the girl had not died but that her spirit rested within another creature.

Matty felt the wind through every quill of her primaries, and then, like an eddy, the air rustled softly through the secondary feathers that grew farther back on her wings. The fan of tail feathers carved the air behind her. The slightest movement changed the pattern.

You fly well—no hunger traces. A voice in her head spoke and she instantly recognized it as Marigold's.

I can't imagine why not, she replied.

You lost the hunger traces when you molted back there at the abbey, I believe.

Is that what I was doing when I grew so still?

That's the best word—molt—for what happened to you, I think! You have left your body, for now, at least.

Yes, said Matty, and as she spoke she realized precisely what she must do. It all came together quickly and clearly in her mind. With Marigold and her other hawks, she'd fly into the forest of Barnsdale and recover the rubies. They'd take them not to Robin but all the way across the English Channel to France, where Queen Eleanor, mother of King Richard, lived.

We must fly back to the castle mews. I must speak with the others. We will need their help.

A full moon began to rise in the sky as they approached the castle. They followed streams of silver light that seemed to pour directly into the arrow slit windows at the top of the keep's tower. The moonlight made everything so clear that Matty could see a spider against the stone of the tower. She could see every fleck of mica in the rocks.

It's not just the moonlight. You are seeing like a bird now, Marigold explained as she sensed Matty's astonishment. *Now when we get in there, Matty, it might come as a bit of a shock to the others—you being back as part of me. But they are quick to learn. Old Moss, of course, will be most pleased.*

She is all right, old Moss?

She misses you fiercely. But she is a tough old hawk. Her anger at the abbess and the sheriff, I think, has made her stronger. She will murder for you, Matty.

She might have to, Matty replied.

They swept in on a following breeze.

"You're back at last," said Morgana from her perch as Marigold alit.

"Hush up, Morgana!" snapped Lyra. "Something's amiss here. I feel it, feel it from my primaries right down to my barbs. Feel it in my rachis! Something is odd."

"She's here, isn't she?" Old Moss spoke. "Matty, you're here, aren't you?"

"Yes, dear, I'm here."

"We have heard such terrible tales, child. No one knows whether you are dead or alive. Of course, Marigold told us you were alive. You know Fynn—he's quite good to us. Brings us food, takes the others out on his fist to hunt. No one could have ever predicted he had the makings of a falconer as a child. I shall never forget how you had him try to fly me once years ago. I think it was on the feast of Saints Simon and Jude, or maybe 'twas the day before on the feast of Saint Odhran.

"Oooh, Moss, do stop it with this endless chatter," Morgana whined.

"Don't be short, Morgana," Matty reprimanded the kestrel.

"Matty, is that you?" Morgana asked. "I'm confused."

"Yes," Marigold and Matty both answered.

"She's part of me, Morgana," Marigold said. "And that doesn't change things a whit. She is still our mistress."

"So, Matty," said Lyra, "why are you here and, if I may be so bold, why in this form?"

"Well, now, you wouldn't expect her to come as

a hoofed creature, would you—a cow or a goat or a horse?" Moss said.

"How ridiculous! Not our Matty," offered Ulysses in his slow, meditative voice.

"And what did you do with your other self?" Morgana asked.

"That's difficult to explain," Marigold chimed in. "Her body lies in the abbey, seemingly close to death, while her spirit is free."

"But—" Matty spoke quite softly now. The birds grew still on their perches. "It is only temporary, my friends. I could slip either way. I had decided that my last sanctuary was death. I know that you of all creatures understand this the best." At those words each of the magnificent birds nodded. "But there is more at stake than my own life. There is the life of our country. Our king has been kidnapped. And now is the time for us to fly to the greenwood. . . . I understand now what you tried to explain before about the earth points—the two earth points. I feel them in my head, just as you must."

Moss grew terribly excited. "You feel the *nwamelk*, Matty? The pull of the north point?"

"Yes. It was as if I lived in a flat world before and

now I feel the shape of this world. . . . It's as if I feel the shine of the stars in my hollow bones, the pull of the moon on my brain, the earth points in my gizzard."

"When do we leave?" Ulysses asked. "What is the battle strategy?" Erect on his perch, his tufted shoulders squared, he appeared like a knight ready to receive his orders from his monarch.

"We go now." Matty addressed the bird. "We'll recover the rubies, but before that there is something here I must get."

"What's that?" Morgana asked.

Matty turned to Moss.

"It's still there, Matty. Don't worry." The old peregrine made her way painfully to the dust bath trough and poked deep into the sand. When she lifted her head, Matty saw the Star of Jerusalem glittering in her beak.

"Yes," Lyra said, "we're good at keeping secrets."

"I know," Matty replied. "So then, with the sapphire, once we get the rubies, we can fly on."

"Fly on to where?" Lyra asked.

"Across the Channel, to France. To Queen Eleanor."

Then Marigold spoke. "The winds are from the

west. We can make it within the space of a day and another night."

"But, Matty," Moss said in a quavering voice, "you know my vision is gone, my talons shrunk. My flight feathers are a mess. I molt only very occasionally. The last time—when was it? Saint Rupert's day? Or am I off entirely? Was it a summer molt or the feast of Saint Alban? I will go, but I am not the strongest of fliers."

"It does not matter, dear." Matty spoke gently. "For this flight I will be with you." Matty knew the time had come to switch from Marigold to Moss. Once again Matty began to feel a pushing in her brain, and just as her spirit had meshed with Marigold's it began to interweave with Moss's. It was as if Moss were the warp and Matty the weft. Together they made a single cloth.

And suddenly the old peregrine experienced a peculiar sensation. This was unlike any molt she had ever undergone. Moss felt a tingle as if her feathers were infused with a new life and energy. There was a prickling and then a deep pain as her talons lengthened. The bird blinked, and for the first time in years Moss could see clearly. She roused her wings. A surge of new energy coursed through her.

Not yet, Matty's voice within her head cautioned.

Matty, I feel as fresh as a young eyas, Moss said, referring to the young hawks.

But I am counting on your older instincts, Moss, Matty replied. *You taught me once how to be a falconer. Now you must teach me to be a bird of prey, a raptor!*

Chapter 34

WINGS AT DAWN

Short-winged hawks, or true hawks, fly low and kill by stealth; falcons fly high and plunge to kill. Thus, falcons are well adapted because of their methods for prey in clearings and fields.

AGAINST THE PALE PINK of the dawn five great-winged birds rose in flight. The birds' primary feathers glinted with a rosy luster as they caught the first rays of the sun.

"I feel completely re-imped from head to talons!" Moss said. "And my vision!"

Matty herself was astonished by the splendor of this flight at dawn. The minute adjustments of Moss's flight feathers enabled them to pass through the air effortlessly so she could ride thermal updrafts, to glide, to hover.

In no time they were over the greenwood of Barnsdale, and she had quickly spotted half a dozen royal foresters. *And just imagine we are about to steal the treasure right out from under them!* Matty thought gleefully.

"All right, bear north," she commanded the others. "The first tree is a spruce. There it is, below. Moss and I land first. Marigold, there is an oak directly behind it. Take the others there and you'll find a nest in a hollow on the east side." But Marian was not exactly sure if she had spoken the words *north* or *east*. She was aware of this new way of thinking about direction, aware of the slight pull in her brain toward an earth point. What talk there occurred between the birds was rather brief. "Moss and I will meet you, and then we'll go on to the next trees that are a bit harder to find."

Moss settled onto a large branch of the spruce. *Now, Moss, close to where this branch joins the trunk,* Matty said, *there's a hollow above.* They quickly lofted the short distance. Matty blinked as Moss poked her head into the hole. *It looks like a nest!* the peregrine said.

We wrapped each ruby in moss and dried grass.

She felt Moss's beak tearing gently at a clump at the bottom of the hollow. Suddenly there was a bright flicker of red. *That's it!* they both said at once. *Now can you hold it in your beak? And now hold the sapphire in your talon?*

Certainly, Moss replied, and clamped her beak onto the ruby.

They met the other birds at the oak and Moss, with Matty as guide, led on.

As they settled in the last tree to pluck the fifth ruby, a royal forester came tromping down the path. He looked up and might have briefly wondered why five hawks had gathered in one tree. The birds felt their gizzards freeze. "What's he doing?" Morgana asked.

"Just stay still," Matty cautioned.

"I'll fight if I have to," Ulysses said.

"No, not yet. Just stay still," Matty repeated. The forester stood there, studying the hawks. He looked nervously at the leper tree and its scaly leaves; then he simply walked on. A feeling of great relief swept through the birds. "Lyra, that last one is yours," Matty said.

"The ocean!" Matty cried. Ahead was the Channel dividing England from Europe. It boiled with white-caps in the gusty winds. The wind had turned, and the tailwind was boosting their speed and making the flight much less tiring. By late afternoon they were in France.

"Where is the queen?" Marigold asked.

"Barfleur," Matty replied. On the old map of her father's he'd once marked the fields where he had fought when he was a young knight with Hodge as his squire. Barfleur was near Cherbourg, the port town where he had first set foot on French soil after crossing the Channel. She remembered exactly where the town was—west of the river Seine in a notch on the coast of Normandy. She could picture the map so clearly in her mind, but it was no longer simply a flat drawing. She felt its position precisely in reference to the *nwamelk,* and, as she did, she noticed that the sensation transmitted itself to Moss, who was flying the point position.

They had been flying over the water for not more than an hour when the peregrine began to carve a banking turn. The other birds followed. Now flying parallel to the coast they continued in a southerly direction. The sun had already set and twilight engulfed them in a fragile purple light.

Spotting the turrets, Matty exclaimed suddenly, "That must be it! I see a castle!"

Chapter 35

THE PEREGRINE AND THE QUEEN

Falconry—art or sport? Perhaps both. But the more popular it becomes, one fears that the less of an art it will be. And yet to think of it as mere blood sport is a disservice to the true falconer and, of course, the hawks.

So THE PEREGRINE, GUIDED by Matty, swept through the courtyard and the various gardens of the castle of Barfleur. The other birds waited on a courtyard wall. The castle was not much bigger than her father's and the plan was quite similar. By now it was night, and Matty could tell that most of the candles and torches had been extinguished, but in a small building on the castle grounds she saw something bright hanging in the night like an illuminated flower. It possessed an enchanting, almost eerie beauty. *It's a window!* Matty thought. *A stained-glass window. So this must be the chapel, Moss, and someone must be inside.*

Quietly Moss flew into the building through a small arched entrance.

The peregrine perched between two arches. Below, an elderly woman was kneeling. Her head was wrapped in a tight coif anchored on top by a simple gold crown.

This is the queen! Can we get closer, Moss, without being seen?

In a shadowy corner was a stone statue of the Madonna. Moss flew and landed on her shoulder. There was a tiny click as the sapphire ring Moss held in her talon touched the stone. The queen turned her head slightly. Had she heard them? The light from one of the tapers illuminated her profile. She had been crying. She turned her head back toward the altar and continued to pray.

Go with the jewels, Moss. The bird lofted herself into the air and flew toward the queen. Now the woman turned and gave a little shriek as she saw the wingspread of the old peregrine. But then she caught sight of the gleaming jewel in the talon. Her flinty gray eyes suddenly sparkled. And when Moss landed directly in front of her, she leaned in closer, so close Matty could see every line in the woman's face. Her cheekbones were high and a spray of pale freckles scattered across them. The strands of hair that poked out from beneath her coif were more brownish than gray. Matty thought she had probably once had fiery red hair like King Richard.

Matty had never been this close to a queen, and this queen did not even suspect that one of her son's loyal subjects now perched before her. Moss dipped her head in a gesture of deep reverence and dropped the sapphire into the soft folds of the hem of the queen's gown.

"God be praised." The queen at first did not touch the jewel. She looked down at it as if the stone had fallen directly from heaven. "A star sapphire! The Star of Jerusalem!" She picked up the jewel. Her fingers were gnarled, her knuckles swollen. She opened her mouth, but no sound came as she glimpsed the twinkling at the sapphire's center. Then Moss dropped a ruby. Now the queen gasped and looked into the old peregrine's eyes. In that moment Matty felt a connection. *She senses me. I know it. She senses that there is something human within this bird. She was praying for a miracle for her son Richard and now she believes it has come. Well, it has!*

A fine web of lines radiated from the corners of the old queen's flinty eyes. Though spots stained her forehead, she was still a handsome woman. She tipped her head to the side and looked into Moss's eyes. There was a current, a pulse, like an invisible filament that sparked between the woman and the bird. The queen herself had been a falconer as a young girl and knew the way of hawks.

The queen's voice creaked like a rusted hinge as she began to speak aloud. "I do not presume to know everything, but I know that what stands before me is more than a bird." Her jaw trembled slightly. "Is this to do with my son? With Richard?"

Moss nodded. And then, extending her talons, she gently touched the woman's hand. Queen Eleanor's eyes swam with confusion. She had never been touched by a creature in such a way. It was such a quintessentially human gesture, telling her to be calm, not to fear, to be patient. The peregrine then spread her wings and flew out of the church the way she had entered. Eleanor turned to follow the bird's flight. As old Moss passed through the high-arched opening, she emitted four shrill cries.

"The peregrine is calling others!" Queen Eleanor clasped the two gems in her hand. "I know that call. I know it."

She waited tensely and soon she heard wingbeats. The peregrine reappeared, followed by a goshawk, a kestrel, a short-winged hawk, and a lovely little merlin with bright flecks of gold in its dark eyes. Each one dipped in a gesture of deep reverence and released a ruby. The five stones seemed to possess a life of their own, throbbing like five small hearts. The red glister of the light within them tinged the darkness of the chapel with a luminous glow.

"You have brought me a king's ransom, a ransom for my son!" Tears streamed down the queen's face. "Richard shall be free!"

Matty marveled for, like Moss, the old queen seemed mysteriously to become less frail. Something quickened in her. Her once-trembling hands grew steady.

That night a message was taken to the Holy Roman Emperor, who now held King Richard—a message delivered not by an ambassador but by Moss.

"What the devil?" the very emperor shouted as the peregrine flew into his audience chambers. He threw up his arms, for it appeared as if the bird were about to attack him. *Drop it now,* Matty commanded. There was a solid thunk as the ruby wrapped in cloth dropped at the emperor's feet. A page bent to retrieve it.

"What is it?"

"I'm not sure, your majesty," the page said.

"Well, find out."

It tried the emperor's patience to wait for the twine to be unwrapped.

He gasped, then whispered a mighty oath as he saw the sparkling ruby that lay at the center of the cloth.

"There's a note with it, your majesty."

"Yes, yes." The emperor picked up a small furled piece of parchment. "A message from Queen Eleanor of England," he whispered.

The emperor's minister had come to his side. "What does she write?"

"'Sir, there are four more rubies equal to this one and the magnificent Star of Jerusalem, thus constituting a price far greater than your ransom of one hundred and fifty thousand marks. Send your ambassadors with my son and they shall be yours.' It is signed: Eleanor."

Chapter 36

HAWK FEVER

Bathing a hawk's feet in water distilled from lettuces,
nightshade, or juice of the henbane root can relieve a
fever.

TIME CAN DO STRANGE things. The days of the
journey to Barfleur and then on to the emperor
were a blur in the mind that Matty and Moss
now shared. The ransom had been delivered. Richard
was released, but it all seemed like a dream. Matty felt
herself and Moss both weakening on their flight back
to England. Was it a fever? A hawk fever? Would the
treatments she had used to cure the birds work for her
and Moss? And even so who would know how to treat
them?

She knew that some unseen power had allowed

her this time out of time, this life that had straddled both living and dying, both human and bird, splicing feather and flesh. But the effort had been great, and she now felt that the end was near. She could hear the others speaking as they flew those last miles back to the Fitzwalter castle.

"Come, Moss, you can make it." Lyra and Ulysses were both flying under the peregrine, creating an updraft so that the bird would not have to pump her wings so vigorously, for each wingbeat seemed to deplete her strength. Matty, too, felt their shared strength ebbing, her heart slowing.

Marigold flew and spoke to them both. "We're almost there. I see the castle. Hang on! Oh, Matty, live!"

"Trying. Trying." The whispered words were not quite bird nor were they human.

They flew in through the window on the east wall of the mews. Moss, too weak to perch, settled on the floor. The other birds brought talons full of straw to pile around her. Matty felt a tearing inside. *We are separating, but I am as withered as this old peregrine.*

"Matty, say something. Say something," Marigold begged. But Matty could say nothing. She watched from somewhere just above Moss. Watched the bird's chest heaving, the breaths growing shallower, the peregrine's eyes no longer seeing. The space between each breath grew longer until . . . until . . .

In the shadows of the cell of the abbey, the lepers gathered around.

"Is she still breathing?" Helena asked.

"Hardly," said a legless old man. "She can't last till morning."

And Marian felt herself dissolving like night dew in the rising sun. She felt no pain. Nothing. *Death is not that bad,* she thought with mild surprise. It seemed almost like an old friend who had waited patiently for her at the end of a very long road. Had she the strength, she would have run to it. *Yes, I am falling in love with dying,* she thought. *In love . . .*

"She's gone, isn't she?" Morgana said as she looked at the unmoving feathers on the floor of the mews.

"Yes," Marigold replied. They had all felt it, known it the instant Moss died. It was like a breeze passing through the mews and then only stillness, a whisper, and finally silence. No more. "But Matty—is she gone, too?" The birds began to cock their heads, swiveling them this way and that. There was an emptiness in the mews that none of them had ever experienced. They dared not speak what each one sensed. "Matty?" whispered Marigold. But there was nothing.

"She's not here," Lyra said softly.

Suddenly Marigold felt a great anger suffuse every one of her hollow bones.

"We're going!" she announced.

"Where? What's to be done?" Lyra asked.

"She has to be somewhere," Marigold said staunchly. "This . . ." she said, looking down at the body that had held Moss, "this is not Matty."

Then Ulysses said, "Marigold, you loved her like no other. Because of you she was almost hawk, and because of her you were almost human; but she is gone. She has died."

"But, Ulysses, even in death, she must be *somewhere*. Moss's body is here." Marigold's voice cracked. She could not bear to think of Matty as a body. "Terrible things have been done to her. We cannot right all wrongs. But I swear on the memory of Matty, I will take my vengeance on her enemies."

The three other hawks were suddenly jolted from

their grief. "We fly at daybreak!" Marigold said.

A cacophony of raucous caws filled in the mews.

Below, old Meg turned in her sleep and thought, *Ah yes, Matty must be back stirring up the hawks. Imping their feathers, filing their talons* . . . but then she blinked her eyes, opened them wide, and she realized how silly that was. Matty had been gone for weeks and she knew not where. She was completely alone now in the castle. Hodge had died the day after Matty had disappeared. The loneliness she felt was as sharp and painful as any ache in her stiff old bones.

It had not been more than a few days since Robin had received the message that Marian was being kept at the Nottingham abbey. He did not know all that had transpired since and that her hawks were mourning what they sensed might be her death. Instead, he was merry with an ingenious scheme to free her.

"You see, fellows, it has taken me a while to plan this. But I have gone out and watched that abbey and come to see they do a thriving business in funerals for lepers. So here is my idea." He looked around, his eyes lively. "I propose that we have a leper's funeral . . . but for an uncommon leper."

"Yes," said Rich slowly, a sly twinkle in his eyes. "Do go on? Who is this leper?"

"Me, of course!"

"Oh, this beats all!" Little John whooped. "Can I be the priest?"

"And of course I'll be the friar," said Friar Tuck.

"Yes, and the rest of you the mourners. And call in all the boys—we need lots of mourners. Spread the word that this is a rather well-off leper. They'll swing open the gates for us. Get ready, boys. Time to mourn! And time at last to rescue Marian."

Chapter 37

THE DEATH WALKERS

*It has been said that in the rank of living things hawks
are not below or above humans but share the splendors
of this world and its hardships. They are raptors, but
humans, too, are predators. Nonetheless, these two living
orders can, like nations separated by borders or oceans,
when necessary, help each other.*

"LOOK DOWN THERE." MARIGOLD tipped her head
as they approached the abbey.

"What is it?" Lyra asked.

"Matty's friend, the friar." Her voice broke. "I—I
think it's what humans call a death walk, one they do
for their final ceremonies."

"Final ceremonies?" Ulysses asked.

"Yes, when someone dies. I learned about it those

times I visited Matty at the abbey. They call them funerals. But they also have them for lepers even before they die. And I think this one is for a leper."

"Not Matty?" Morgana said with excitement.

"No. See that limping figure, the one with a crutch. They are bringing him to the abbey. But—but . . ."

"But what?" Ulysses asked.

"There's something about him. I'm not sure. Let me go explore."

Marigold plunged down, then peeled off as she approached the procession so she was hovering just above the straggly line of marchers. She managed to flit through the line and peer deeply into the hooded face of the limping man. "Marigold!" Robin exclaimed. Next to him in the garb of a priest was the towering figure of Little John and then Rich. Behind them, dressed as monks and mourners, were many more of Robin's men.

Marigold flew back to the other hawks. "It is Robin Hood!" She swiveled her head toward the goshawk. "Ulysses, now that Moss is gone, you fly point the best. We need to support the death walkers. There will be an attack, I am sure."

"All right!" Ulysses cawed, like the voice of

a commander, experienced in battle. "Form up. Marigold, fly port flank. Lyra, fly starboard. Morgana, follow them."

The abbess stood erect at the gates of the abbey. She wondered briefly why it was not the usual priest heading the procession. Well, no matter. She had been told that one of these lepers was quite well off and with no heirs. It would be easy to confiscate his money and possessions.

As the procession filed into the courtyard and finally into the chantry, the abbess did not notice the four birds hovering in the sky.

The trestles in the chantry were draped with the black cloth. The leper began to kneel for his last confession. The service had just begun when Will, shrouded in his monk's habit, slipped in beside Robin. "A contingent of sheriff's men on the way. News of your wealth, I think, has spread a bit wider than we might like. Seems that the sheriff wants to get the same share as his sister."

"Sibling squabbles. How tiresome. Are we outnumbered?"

"About even."

"Fear not, we've got the birds on our side. That puts us ahead."

The service was brief. It was time for the symbolic burial. The abbess stood by the priest as he prepared to sprinkle the dirt on the leper's feet. "Thou art dead to the living, but alive again to God."

Suddenly the leper's black shroud swirled into the air. "By the bishop's buttocks, I'm dead!" roared Robin Hood, flashing his sword. The abbess swayed. Her mouth pulled into a grimace of disbelief. The other mourners were instantly transformed. Rich and Scarlet tore off their dark clothes and stood in the green of the men of Sherwood Forest. Through the chantry doors burst Little John.

Then, seemingly from nowhere, a forward guard of the sheriff's men began swarming into the outer courtyard of the abbey.

"We have a fight on our hands, lads," Robin shouted. More men in green rushed over the courtyard walls. Robin turned to his followers "Listen to me, men of Sherwood. Head for the rooftop. Fit shafts to your bows and aim for their hearts. And now, milady"— he addressed the abbess, who was stunned beyond speech—"kindly direct us to your prisoner."

The abbess remained silent. "You are a common thief."

"And so are you! God's kneecaps, woman, do you hear me! Take me to Marian," Robin roared. He glimpsed the flash of metal just as she dragged a dagger from within her robes and raised it to slash his throat.

The four hawks caught the glint of the dagger and, as if one, they hurled toward the figure. Marigold had never flown with such fury. She thrust her legs forward and extended her murderous talons. A bloodcurdling scream ripped from the abbess's throat. Her hands were useless to protect her from the bird's brutal attack. Fingers were broken, and then the abbess's translucent eyes were gouged out. In one quick slash of the talons her throat was cut. The abbess collapsed to the ground.

"Marigold," Ulysses commanded, "you and Morgana stay here. Lyra and I will meet the sheriff's force on the road." Instantly, Ulysses and Lyra were flying in low passes over the sheriff's men. They aimed for throats and heads, knocking the men off their horses more by surprise than force.

Inside the courtyard Marigold and Morgana

continued to wreak havoc while Robin hurried toward the leper hospital with Little John at his side.

Robin plunged into the room with its wreckage of humanity, and his blood ran cold. There on a pallet lay Marian, barely breathing, her face the color of stone. Nearby was a heap of bones with a few fragments of flesh remaining wrapped in a shroud. From that heap came a voice.

"She is not living, but she is not dead. She is elsewhere, Robin. She has shed this body for now, as one might leave their clothes. Do not fear. Gather her close, and take her to the greenwood, once more to the blasted oak of Sherwood."

Chapter 38

YARAK!

Never discard a molted feather or a broken one. For imping, a falconer needs a good supply so that the best selection might be made for the closest match.

ARIAN HAD BEEN so close, so far down the road, and her old friend Death had been waiting, when suddenly it was as if that friend turned away. "But Moss . . . you took Moss. . . . Why not me? I'm tired . . . so tired I don't want to go on!" Death paused, and Marian felt hope. But then Death said, almost casually, looking over her shoulder, "It's not your time!" and walked on without a backward glance.

Still Marian tried to argue. "It is my time!"

"Live, Marian! Live! Please live! I love you. You can't die."

Someone was kneeling by her. He had been there for days, possibly weeks, crying, begging her not to die. Now for the first time since she had been rescued, Marian's eyelids fluttered open.

"Robin? Robin, it's you?"

"Yes. Me."

"How long have I been this way?"

"More than a fortnight. Marian, there is much to live for. Richard has been freed. He makes his way back to England."

"Then it worked. The ransom worked."

"You made it work. You and your hawks. You see, you must live. I love you."

Marian felt a glad thrill in her weakened heart. In a voice that was barely a whisper she said, "Then you must imp me back to health."

"What do I do?"

"You must hunt me a hare and make a rich broth from its flesh and at first feed it to me slowly. And my ankles that are sore and bloody from the jesses, you must bathe them in a tincture of henbane and water of lettuce and just a touch of nightshade. Then dry them and rub them with balm of aloe."

"And this will make you well, Marian?"

"Oh yes, Robin. And I shall love you forever and ever." They were now beyond words and could only peer so deeply into each other's eyes that, for them, all the world disappeared.

At that moment Little John came into the blasted oak. His eyes brimmed with joy.

"Robin, at last!"

Robin looked up at his old friend. "He's back, truly?"

Little John nodded. "Truly, and he wants to see Marian."

"She is too weak."

"He insists."

"Insists?"

"I would not argue. I think he has the right."

"Then bring him in, but tell him he cannot stay for long."

The shadow of a tall man sliced across the hollow, and there was the clank of metal. The man knelt by the animal furs on which Marian rested. "Your majesty!" Marian gasped.

"Milady, I understand you are the reason I am here today. And although precious jewels were the ransom for my own life, *you* are England's most precious jewel."

Marian closed her eyes. She remembered that terrible day when her father had told her mother to hide her. His words came back so clearly it was as if he were right here with her. "Hide. Suzanne! Hide Matty! . . . Forget the jewels. Matty is our only jewel."

She felt the king lean closer to her. "Can she hear me?" he asked.

A trace of a smile crossed her face. She began to speak in a low whisper. Everyone leaned toward her, for she could barely be heard, but it sounded as if she was laughing. "I wouldn't fit in the potato hole." She chuckled.

"Potato hole?" whispered the king.

"She must be talking about the raid on her father's castle. Her parents tried to hide her in a potato hole," Robin said. "But I'm not sure why she is talking about this now. It was so long ago."

"Because I was my father's only jewel," Marian

replied in a much stronger voice.

A wonderful sense of relief swept through the blasted oak. The king now rose. He turned to Robin. "Can you perhaps lift her up a bit?"

Robin put his arm around Marian and, supporting her back, held her so that she was almost sitting. The king drew his sword. He raised it and then tapped her on each shoulder.

"Right mindful of your prowess on the field, I, Richard, king of England, dub thee Lady Marian of the forests of Sherwood and Barnsdale, a knight of the realm."

A knight am I! Oh! thought Marian. *How much nicer to be a knight than a jewel.*

She looked at Robin. She felt a surge deep within her, a new keenness. *Yarak. I am yarak once more!*

EPILOGUE

More than four hundred years later a book was found in the ruins of an ancient castle's library, a book from medieval times. The title was The Art of Falconry: A Compleat Guide to the Principles and Practices of Hawking. *It is thought to be the first book ever written on hawking by a woman. The author's name was Marian Greenleaf. The book was dedicated "To Moss, Marigold, Ulysses, Lyra, Morgana, my greatest teachers, and to Robin, my greatest love."*

GLOSSARY

THE BIRDS

MORGANA: Kestrel, a small hawk, also known as a sparrow hawk or a killy hawk, because its high-pitched call sounds like *killy killy*. It is grouped with the longwing hawks.

ULYSSES: Goshawk, a medium to large hawk, one of the fastest and most lethal trained hawks. Skilled at maneuvering through dense forests.

LYRA: Shortwing, a true hawk of the genus *Accipiter*, with short, rounded wings and light eyes.

MARIGOLD: Merlin, a small falcon, known as a strong flier. Merlins have horny teeth, which prove effective in tearing flesh of prey. Difficult to train.

MOSS: Peregrine, large, about the size of a crow. Considered the fastest animal in the world. With its long wings, it can achieve speeds of more than two hundred miles per hour.

NOTES

taken by Matty Fitzwalter, daughter of Lord William Fitzwalter,

during her recovery in the winter of 1187

BATE: To attempt to fly off the hand or perch when held or tied.

EYAS: A nestling or young hawk taken from a nest.

FALCON: A female peregrine, also used for females of other species of hawks.

HAGGARD: A hawk trapped when it is mature.

HOOD: A close-fitting leather hood is used to blindfold a hawk.

IMP: A method of repairing broken flight feathers by replacing the broken section with part of another feather.

IMPING NEEDLE: A splint used to join the two parts of a broken feather.

JESSES: The narrow strips of leather placed around a hawk's leg to hold it tethered.

LONGWINGS: All falcons that have long, pointed wings and dark eyes, like Morgana.

LURE: An imitation bird or animal used to attract a hawk in training.

QUARRY: The game, or prey, that is the object of a hawk's hunt.

RING UP: To climb in a spiral flight.

RINGING FLIGHT: When a hawk rings up, chasing quarry.

SHORTWING: A true hawk of the genus *Accipiter*, with short, rounded wings and light-colored eyes, like Lyra.

SOAR: When a hawk flies for the fun of it, gliding on thermals and air currents rather than chasing prey.

STOOP: Diving descent of a longwing attacking with wings nearly closed.

TIERCEL: The male peregrine, which is a third smaller than the female. The term is often misused for the male of any species of hawk.

WAIT ON: To wait in flight high over the falconer.

WEATHER: To place the hawk on her block in open air during the day.

YARAK: Fit, keen, and ready to be flown.

AUTHOR'S NOTE

W as there really an outlaw named Robin Hood who became the hero to the people of England during the lawless rule of Prince John? Was there a Maid Marian? A Little John? There are as many theories about the Robin Hood legends as grains of sand in an hourglass. Although this prince of thieves and his merry band of outlaws purportedly lived during the late twelfth century, the legends and ballads of their exploits did not become popular until the fifteenth and sixteenth centuries as part of May Day celebrations. Some said that Robin and Marian were woodland gods who were celebrated at these revels. Other scholars have suggested that the Robin Hood character was based on a real nobleman—an earl, no less—the Earl of Huntington; while some say he was a farmer named Robyn Hoode. He has also been known as Robin of Locksley, Robehod, Hobbehod, and as a fisherman called Simon over the Lee. His occupation has changed over the years. In the earliest ballads that appeared between 1200 and 1400, he was said to be a yeoman. By the time of Elizabeth I, he had become an earl. He was always, however, a robber.

The other Merry Men also had, at one time or another, slightly different names. Will Scarlet, it is said, was originally called Will Scarloke, Scadlock, or Scathelok. Little John was said to have been John Little or John of Hathersage or John Naylor or John the Nailer. Rich Much had sometimes been called Midge.

In the earliest Robin Hood stories, there was no Maid Marian. There was no Friar Tuck. Marian began to appear as a character in the May Day celebrations. In some, she was portrayed as a dainty maid, a shepherdess; in other stories, she, too, was of noble origins. She was called a variety of names. Miriam, Mary, the Nut Brown Girl, and Matilda Fitzwalter, the daughter of a baron. In the legends, she has often been portrayed as being as fine an archer as Robin and equally good with a sword. Matty as a falconer was my invention. Falconry itself did not become widespread in England until after the Crusades.

The mists of time mingling with the shadow

of legend have obscured true identities or often transformed them. But nevertheless, the tales endure and fascinate. For my own story, I decided to take shreds of various legends and of real history. It was my notion that Robin and Marian and some of his Merry Men had known each other as children, played together, and found solace and inspiration in the greenwood of Barnsdale near the supposed birthplace of Robin Hood. I wanted to know them, imagine them as boys and girls—spirited, mischievous, but with a keen sense of justice and mistrust of authority and the monarchy that was putting a terrible burden on the people of England.

Despite these mists and shadows, certain elements of my story rest on true historical events. King Richard really had left England in the charge of his brother, John, to fight in the Holy Land. On his return, Richard was captured by Duke Leopold of Austria and held for ransom. Richard's mother, Queen Eleanor, living in Barfleur, France, at the time, was desperate to raise his ransom that was said to be the equivalent of three tons of silver. She had asked for the pope's assistance. Richard was finally released in February 1194. At this time, King Philip of France sent a message to Prince

John that read, "Look to yourself. The devil is loose."

Richard was given a hero's welcome on his return and actually forgave Prince John! In 1199, Richard died. Upon his death, John became king and was as awful as one might anticipate. Because of his abuse of all people's rights, he was confronted by a group of barons with a document that later became known as the Great Charter, or Magna Carta, that forced him to respect certain rights and legal procedures. The Magna Carta is considered one of the most important documents in the history of democracy and certainly influenced the Constitution of the United States and the Bill of Rights that were written more than five hundred years later.

HAWKSMAID

A Q&A with Kathryn Lasky

Why did you choose to retell the story of Robin Hood this way?
I have a penchant for turning stories inside out, upside down, whatever. In short, I like to try and find a fresh perspective from which to tell a familiar story. So at first I thought, *what were Robin Hood, Little John, and Maid Marian like as kids?* And then I wondered, *what if I made Maid Marian the real protagonist in the story, the catalyst?* I felt there could be a real emotional wealth considering the constraints set up for young girls and women in that era—basically the choices were to become a nun or get married!

What was the most difficult aspect about researching and writing *Hawksmaid*?
There was an immense amount of research. First, I had to learn about medieval life in England at that time. How they ate, how they dressed, a lot about the architecture, the history of the time and of course all the information about falconry. That last part I loved researching.

Why do you admire hawks and falcons?
Well, of all birds they are really the keenest flyers and very intelligent. They have some amazing capabilities. For example, peregrine falcons can fly up to eighty miles per hour! It's astounding. Also, the bond between humans and hawks that is forged through falconry is endlessly fascinating to me.

What are some of your favorite books?
Oh, I have so many! *To Kill a Mockingbird*, of course. Almost

anything by Edith Wharton—*The Age of Innocence* and *The Custom of the Country* in particular.

I also love Jane Austen and the mystery writer James Lee Burke. I loved Lois Lowry's book *The Giver*.

What advice do you have for aspiring authors?
Keep reading! Good literature encourages a suppleness of mind.

As you read, notions of syntax, narrative forms, and hero arcs are embedded in your mind. So I would say the best advice I can give an aspiring author is read all you can for pleasure.

The Real Sherwood Forest

Though scholars continue to debate whether or not Robin Hood existed—and what his true identity was—there is one aspect of the legend that's not up for debate: the existence of Sherwood Forest.

The real Sherwood Forest is located in Nottinghamshire, England. The former royal hunting forest is much smaller today than it would have been in Robin Hood's time. All that remains is approximately 1.63 square miles of forest, a sliver of its former self—though this same sliver of forest has existed since the end of the Ice Age!

One of its ancient trees is the famous Major Oak. Many hundreds of years old, the tree's massive limbs have to be supported by a careful system of beams so that it doesn't collapse under its own weight. This tree is rumored to have been Robin Hood's principal hideout. To avoid capture, all the outlaw had to do was duck inside its hollow trunk! There are several theories about how the tree grew to its enormous size, the most popular being that, hundreds of years ago, three or four smaller trees began to grow close to one another, eventually forming an enormous oak.

The majestic beauty of Sherwood Forest attracts half a million tourists annually, from all around the world.

The Life of a Young Noble Girl

In addition to her ability to communicate with her father's birds, Matty grew up in very special circumstances. When her father lost all his wealth, she was able to avoid some of the harsher realities that came with being a young noble woman in the Middle Ages.

Even before a noble child's birth, parents in the Middle Ages began making arrangements for the future. They chose wet nurses to feed the baby, and dry nurses, who were tasked with other duties, such as rocking the cradle.

Though young girls might have been allowed to play and learn with their brothers, once they reached six or seven years old, they found themselves separated. The boys had male tutors, who taught them reading and writing, and they were also trained in hunting, horsemanship, and weaponry. By twelve or fourteen, these same boys would have begun to receive lessons on knighthood, including how to wear armor. They'd learn to handle swords and lances, and perhaps participate in jousting tournaments.

Girls, on the other hand, were educated in a very different manner. A noble woman was selected to supervise the young girl's upbringing, ensuring she would grow up under the strict code of morality and good manners expected of the nobility. At a young age, they were usually sent away from home to receive schooling, either in a monastery or in another castle. There, they were taught "household" duties, such as manners, dancing, sewing, reading and writing Latin, singing, and other skills that would allow her to run a house and entertain guests in the future. These young girls were essentially expected to act as servants to the older ladies of the castle and monasteries they were sent to.

Though Matty's circumstances are truly tragic, her gifts with the hawks and falcons and her family situation allowed her to avoid the two most typical fates of young women in the Middle Ages: marriage or joining a convent. Some young ladies were engaged to be married as young as six or seven years old, especially if their parents aimed to use the marriage to seal political ties or obtain greater wealth. Girls were usually married by the time they turned fourteen!

THE LAST MUSKETEER

by STUART GIBBS

"What's wrong, Greg? You've always wanted to visit Paris!"

Greg turned from the cab window and frowned at his cheerful mom, squished in the backseat beside him. He'd been watching the tour boats on the Seine River, crammed full of tourists gaping at the Eiffel Tower, all with equally cheerful faces.

"Yeah, but on vacation," he couldn't help but point out.

"This *is* a vacation," his father replied.

"I guess." Greg wasn't sure. Being forced to sell all your

1

possessions in order to survive didn't really seem to him to be very vacation-like. On the other hand, maybe his mom and dad *would* cash in and the three of them would all live happily ever after. That's what his parents kept repeating, over and over and over. And Greg wanted to believe it. He really did. Otherwise . . . well, it was best not to think about the alternative.

Dad reached across Mom and patted Greg's shoulder. Greg's father was built like a twig, tall and thin, with dark, wavy hair that always got messed up in the wind. "I admit, we're not here for the best reasons, but that doesn't mean we can't have some fun," he said. "Look, there's the Pont Neuf! The oldest bridge in Paris. It was built more than four hundred years ago!"

"Neat," Greg said. He meant it, but the word came out as more of a groan.

"Come on, Greg," Mom said soothingly. She had dressed to impress today, wearing her most expensive dress and her tallest heels, her blond hair so shellacked with hair spray Greg figured he could probably bounce a rock off it. "We're going to the Louvre right now! The greatest museum in the world. And *we're* getting a private tour!"

"But did we really have to sell *everything* to get it?" Greg asked quietly.

Mom and Dad sighed.

Greg turned back to the window and caught his own

reflection in it. Like his parents, he was thin and pale, with thick brown curls—but he was short for fourteen, and right now his dark brown eyes looked like a sad puppy's. Yikes. He shifted his gaze back to the passing scenery. Around the curve of the Seine, he could see the Louvre ahead. It was impossible to miss: an ornate palace that took up several city blocks with gardens and courtyards. Festooned with carvings and flourishes, it was as much a work of art as the paintings inside. It looked like a giant stone wedding cake.

"It's not like we're *giving* everything away," Greg's father chided. "We are *selling* it. And the museum is being very generous."

"I know," Greg muttered. "Giving up all our stuff really doesn't bother me. I swear. It's just . . . Grandpa Gus always told us we weren't supposed to sell *anything*."

"Then maybe Grandpa Gus shouldn't have squandered so much of the family savings," Greg's mother countered. She had a point.

Out the window, the setting sun turned the Seine a sparkling gold. There was no denying Paris was a beautiful city. Even in his funk, Greg could admit that. If only he could enjoy the trip and could be like those tourists on the boats, but his grandfather's warning kept ringing in his ears.

These heirlooms must always stay in our family, no matter what.

Greg was ten years old when the old man had croaked those words, on one of his famous tours of the family's Connecticut estate. Grandpa Gus had still been living with them, before he got shipped to a nursing home. Everyone else in the family had long ago grown bored of being dragged around the mansion on Sunday afternoons, hearing the same old tales of how the Rich family had come to acquire such magnificent treasures from around the globe. But not Greg, who adored his eccentric grandfather. And on that particular tour, Grandpa Gus had grown uncharacteristically serious. *These things are more important than you can possibly understand,* he'd whispered. *Do whatever it takes to protect them. And most important of all . . .*

"He said we should never take them to France," Greg recalled out loud.

Dad smiled sadly. "He also said his beagle had been George Washington in a former life. The man's compass didn't exactly point due north."

There was a screech of tires behind them, followed by a cacophony of tinny French car horns. Greg spun around. The huge moving truck following them—the one stuffed with all their possessions—had just plowed through a red light, trying to keep up. Cars swerved left and right to avoid it.

"French drivers," Mom remarked with a chuckle. "They're as bad as the Italians."

4

But not nearly as bad as anyone in New York, Greg thought, more depressed than ever. For some reason, the truck reminded him of how much had changed for the worse in the past year, and how far his family had fallen. Recently his whole life seemed to revolve around loading and unloading trucks.

First, his parents had run out of money. Not that this was much of a surprise. For years now, Dad had made no secret that maintaining the family estate cost more than he earned. But when he finally announced, "We're broke," it still came as a shock.

After that, everything had blurred into a routine of selling and moving. So long, Connecticut—where Greg had lived his whole life, where his family had lived for generations, in fact—hello, Queens. So long, beautiful estate—with a duck pond, stables, and a fifty-room mansion—hello, cramped three-room apartment. So long, private school—hello, public.

Mom and Dad couldn't even wait until the end of ninth grade. They had to uproot Greg right in the middle of the year. Which would have been okay. Honestly. He hadn't made any truly close friends with anyone at Wellington Prep. But there was the small matter of making new friends. Back in Connecticut, his skills—horseback riding, fluent French, fencing (he was favored to win the tristate tournament in his age bracket)—had at least made him interesting. At Carver High, they made him a freak. (When Greg had boasted to a girl in his homeroom about his fencing skills, she'd tried to have him arrested for selling stolen property.)

Greg had always felt he wasn't quite like other kids his age, but now everyone at school seemed to share that feeling. On the very first day, a group of bullies had discovered he was reading *20,000 Leagues Under the Sea* in the original French. Worse, they discovered he was reading it just for fun.

They responded by stealing his lunch money and flushing it down the toilet.

Plus, the irony of being named Rich when he no longer was . . . well, even the dumbest kids could make fun of *that*.

But maybe things were turning around. After all, if the Louvre hadn't approached his parents, the "Rich" family (*Ha! Get it?* Greg thought)—well, they might have had to unload everything on eBay.

The museum's interest had come out of the blue. Greg's parents had known their furniture was antique but never expected it might be of historical value. (Grandpa Gus had always insisted it was, but toward the end nobody but Greg took anything Gus said seriously.) And then they'd received a letter from Michel Dinicoeur, the museum's director of Renaissance acquisitions: *"I, Michel Dinicoeur, have discovered that you possess some artifacts of great interest to the Louvre, some of which I have been trying to track down for a very long time. . . ."*

After that, arrangements were made quickly. The museum even footed the bill for plane tickets, the hotel, and shipping everything to France. Greg had hoped the trip would cheer him up, but from the moment he stepped off the plane, he'd been overwhelmed by a sense of foreboding.

His parents had done their best to rouse his spirits, pointing out the famous landmarks on the way in from the airport and enthusiastically making plans for the rest of the week. They'd just spent the afternoon at the Eiffel Tower, even splurging for lunch at the famous Jules Verne restaurant on the second deck. But Greg simply couldn't shake the feeling that Grandpa Gus had known what he was talking about—and that coming to Paris was a terrible mistake.

They passed the Tuileries—acres of formal gardens and spouting fountains—and arrived at the Louvre. The cab began to turn into the central plaza, where I. M. Pei's modern glass pyramid sat above the underground main entrance, a stark contrast to the formal old museum that surrounded it. "Sorry," Greg's father told the driver in French. "We're not tourists. We're going to the loading docks around back."

The cabdriver shrugged, then made a death-defying swerve back into traffic, and continued on the road between the massive museum and the Seine.

"Everything's going to be fine, Greg," Mom said for the hundredth time. She patted Greg's knee, trying to comfort him. But Greg noticed her fingering the silver chain around her neck, something she always did when she was nervous or upset. Her nails absently tapped the black crystal that hung from it.

Greg had never seen his mom without the crystal, even when she exercised. It wasn't a precious stone, and it wasn't even intact—one side was jagged, as though half of it had broken off—but it *was* beautiful and otherworldly. When he was younger, Greg had imagined it might have been a meteorite cast off by a passing comet. Grandpa Gus said it had been in the family going all the way back to their distant ancestor, Cardinal Richelieu, who had been adviser to the kings of France four hundred years ago. But as with everything Gus said, nobody—including Mom herself—seemed to take him seriously. Still, she loved it. Greg's dad had given it to her when he proposed. At least Greg could be certain they wouldn't sell *that* off, and in the midst of his internal upheaval he felt comforted.

The cab rounded the corner of the museum and stopped by a gate where armed guards stood.

The driver turned back to Greg's father, unsure what to do.

Mr. Rich dug into his pocket and pulled another piece

of correspondence from Michel Dinicoeur—including directions and a silver pass. He rolled down the window and handed it to the stone-faced guard, along with the passports of everyone in the family. The guard stepped into a booth, made a phone call to his superior, then returned the passports and raised the gate, waving them through. The cab and the truck plunged down a ramp that led underneath the museum. Greg felt as though he was being swallowed by the earth.

"Isn't this exciting?" his mother asked. "More than eight million people a year visit this museum, and almost none of them get to see this."

"Wow," Greg said, joking. "The loading dock. This is *way* better than the *Mona Lisa*."

"Greg, that's enough," his father said with a tired sigh. "All those years of private school and French tutors and the lessons for horseback riding and fencing and rock climbing . . . They weren't *free*, you know. I don't remember you complaining then."

Greg frowned, ashamed. His father was right. On the other hand, while Greg might have spent some of the family money, he hadn't *lost* any of it. The Riches had been slowly squandering their fortune for over a century, splurging on lousy art and racehorses with bad knees. Even Grandpa Gus was guilty, though he never knew just how much money he'd been wasting.

It didn't really bother Greg that now there would be nothing left to inherit. He wasn't *that* spoiled or selfish. What bothered him was that with all the drastic change in his life, he felt upended, rootless. As though the person he was before no longer existed, or didn't matter. So far he hadn't been able to forge his way into the new life. Would he ever be able to?

The loading area was warm and humid and stank of exhaust fumes. As the cab slowed to a stop, a strange man emerged from the bowels of the building. Greg's eyes narrowed. At first, he wasn't sure if he wanted to laugh or . . . *what*. The man was around thirty, tall and broad-shouldered—with long black hair, a thin mustache, and a small, pointed beard. His clothing wasn't just striking, it was ridiculous. Instead of a suit, he wore breeches, stockings, and a loose-fitting shirt. Greg thought he looked more like an actor on his way to perform Shakespeare than a museum employee. Maybe the people who worked here had to dress up in costume?

"I, Michel Dinicoeur, am pleased to make your acquaintance!" the man cried. He pronounced his own name with an overly dramatic flourish, stressing each syllable as though it was in italics: *Me-shell Di-Ni-coo-rre.* "Welcome to the Louvre!"